SIN
NEVER
SLEEPS

A GILT NOVEL

IVY ESTATE PUBLISHING + ENTERTAINMENT

Cover Image © Bigstock ©Nuttawut Uttamaharad Quantity sales. Special discounts are available on quantity purchases by corporations, associations, and others. For details, contact the "Special Sales Department" at the address above.

Gilt: Sin Never Sleeps/ Geneva Lee.

Electronic ed. ISBN-13 978-1-945163-05-0

Print ed. ISBN-13 978-1-945163-20-3

SIN
NEVER
SLEEPS

A GILT NOVEL

GENEVA LEE

IVY ESTATE

Also by Geneva Lee

THE ROYALS SAGA

Command Me

Conquer Me

Crown Me

Crave Me

Covet Me

Capture Me

Complete Me

THE GOOD GIRLS DON'T SERIES

Novels

Catching Liam

Teaching Roman

Reaching Gavin

Novellas

Unwrapping Liam

STANDALONES AND NOVELLAS

The Sins That Bind Us

Two Week Turnaround

Later

Lies are so easy to tell, and sins are so hard to forgive. It's odd how even something as simple as a coat of paint can be deceptive until viewed in the right light. I never knew what I preferred—a pretty lie or a sorry sinner—until now.

The room has been redone to have a sleek, modern appeal. Everything is white and minimal with clean lines and the most abstract of abstract art, but the stale scent of cigarette smoke still hangs in the room. It's proof that Vegas is a city out of time, or maybe just one unhinged from reality. If it weren't for the acrid smell assaulting my nostrils, the space might actually seem luxurious. No doubt the renovation had been a ploy to try to convince visitors the hotel is worth the hefty price tag.

Next month, I will have some serious explaining to do when my mom and Hans get my emergency credit card bill. But if this situation doesn't count as a crisis, nothing ever will.

I sit on the edge of the bed and wait with my hands folded in my lap. Being nervous is strange. Of course, I've never called a service before. Until a few days ago, my only contact with call girls had been my shoes on the fliers littering the streets. Somehow it still feels inevitable. I'm in too deep not to follow the clues.

But *this* room, in *this* hotel, in *this* city could never hope to be more than a mirage. Because the one thing tourists never see is the truth. The bones of Las Vegas are rotten, weakened by greed and excess. Even in a fancy hotel room I can't see past that fact.

A knock on the door startles me, and I stand, smoothing my dress as if I need to impress her. When I open the door, I'm met by familiar, if surprised eyes. The shock mirrored in them quickly shifts to anger.

Stepping to the side, I hold out my arm. "Won't you come in?"

Chapter 1

"DON'T FORGET YOUR SUNSCREEN," Mom calls to me from across the patio. She eyes me watchfully from under the black brim of an oversized sun hat.

If only this were about sunscreen. I sigh and pick up the bottle of SPF 50 she sets out for me every morning. Slathering it on my legs, I'm careful to avoid the cuts that are still healing from *the incident*, as she calls it.

It's only 10 a.m., but I've already reapplied twice. That's Palm Springs for you. If you don't melt in the sun, your sunscreen will. In some ways, the desert city is a lot like Vegas, particularly when it comes to their heat indexes. But what had once been the exclusive playground to Hollywood is now more of a retirement community.

There isn't much to do here, which is why I like to visit. It's a break from the frenetic hustle of Las

Vegas. But given the circumstances of my early exodus to my mother's house, she's been constantly hovering. It's like having a bodyguard without the perks of being a rock star. No sex, drugs, or rock-n-roll under her watch.

Lying back on the chaise, I shut my eyes tightly to the sun, which is creeping steadily toward the center of the sky. I can still feel its heat as its blazing light burns through my eyelids.

Palm Springs is my place to relax—at least it usually is. But Zen is in short supply these days. On the glass table next to me, my phone buzzes. I don't have to look at the message to know who it's from. There are only two people in the world who would bother to text me, and one of them used his one phone call weeks ago to reach someone else. I can't exactly blame him. After he was arrested for assaulting my father, the police had held him while they continued to investigate his father's murder. Without a law degree, I'm useless to Jameson West. It's been even harder to be supportive since my mother whisked me from the hospital straight to California. Between my absence and my paranoia that he might be a murderer, I'm a shoo-in for girl-friend of the year.

My dad didn't object to the rearrangement of custody, but he'd been avoiding me since our last father-daughter brawl. So I know the text is from neither of them, which only leaves Josie. Pushing myself up, I catch the strings of my bikini top and tie it tightly around my neck. I grab my sunglasses and my phone, but as soon as my feet hit the searing heat of the cement, Mom's face appears from under her hat.

"Drink some water," she advises.

"I will," I promise, forcing myself not to sound too sarcastic. If she doesn't ease up, I'll make good on that promise by drowning myself. The weight of the water would be a lot less oppressive than her nagging.

She's scared, a small voice in my head reminds me.

That makes two of us, another retorts.

Great. Now my inner monologues are fighting, too.

I pause near the sliding glass doors and for a second, the sound of shattering glass and the sharp sting of shards piercing through skin overtakes me. The memory overrides the present until I shake it off.

"Everything okay, Emma?" Mom asks.

I swallow before I nod. "Everything is fine, but I wanted to talk to you about something."

She abandons Oprah's latest book club pick and turns to face me. "Yes?"

"It's just...I promised Dad that I would be around this summer..." I begin, leaving out that I no longer feel obliged to keep that promise—not after I'd been the unintended recipient of his fist. I self-consciously stroke the yellow remnants of the bruise he'd given me. He might have been aiming for Jameson, but he got me. Conveniently for him, no one questioned where the injury on my stomach came from after the accident that night. "So I think I need to head back to Belle Mère."

Her lips purse as if my words taste funny, and she shakes her head slowly. "I don't think that's a good idea. With everything going on there—"

"That's exactly why I need to go back," I interrupt. She had to know this was coming. I've never stayed at her resort in Palm Springs longer than two weeks. As of today, I've been here almost a month. "I've been here a lot longer than usual."

"And you spent the first week on narcotics," she reminds me.

"I'm fine now." I cross my tan arms over my chest, my golden skin serving as further proof that I've spent enough time lounging poolside.

"And you haven't outstayed your welcome," she says as if that's the reason I'd feel obliged to go.

"Look, Josie needs me. The shop needs me—" I stop myself before I add Jameson to that list. Mom doesn't need to know that he is also pulling home, not after what happened at his house. Honestly, I'm not even certain he wants me to return to Belle Mère.

And my Mom may not want to admit it, but the

strange events plaguing my small community concern her. It doesn't take a degree in psychology to know she's choosing to avoid the reality of the situation.

She pulls off her hat and wipes sweat from her damp forehead, then turns the full intensity of her gaze on me. Meeting her cold, emerald eyes is like staring into a mirror. "Hans and I have been talking. We think it would be best if you transfer here for your senior year."

"Here?" I ask in disbelief. "What happened to 'I need to worry about college'? Does Palm Springs even have—"

"Here as in California. There are plenty of options in Los Angeles," she stops me.

"Los Angeles?" I explode. "No way. You might not like it, but I have a life back in Belle Mère."

"A life you almost lost," she says flatly.

"It was an accident," I remind her, even as a shiver ripples up my spine. I'd been too freaked out to tell her the truth, so I'd gone along with the story that Monroe West had concocted about that night. Leighton had been drunk, and when she stumbled, she took me with her, falling through a plate-glass window a few feet to the patio below. I'm certain it was easier to buy off the cops to overlook the underage drinking and partying than it would've been to undermine an investigation into something more sinister. No one has questioned the story, even though Leighton is still in a coma.

But I can't deny the truth to myself: we'd been pushed. Mom didn't know that. Theoretically, Monroe didn't either, even though she'd conveniently fed a story to the paramedics.

"Accidents aren't always innocent," Mom says. The shiver running through me turns into a full chill that settles deeply in my bones. She isn't talking about me and what happened at the West penthouse. She's talking about Becca.

"I'm going to be fine," I promise her softly. I only hope I can make good on that claim.

"We'll talk about this later." She picks her book back up and returns her attention to the dog-eared page. I've been dismissed, but I'm not free to go.

"WHEN ARE YOU COMING HOME?" Josie asks as soon as FaceTime connects. Half of her head is covered in Bantu knots while the rest of her hair is recklessly curly. Josie, like her hair, is a study in contrasts. Both prim and responsible with a wild streak that carves a bigger path through her personality with each passing year. I plop onto my bed with my computer.

"Hello to you, too." The glare of afternoon sun makes it hard to see the screen, so I shimmy toward the headboard.

"It's a serious question, Em. I need you to come home. I need your help."

Her panic raises my eyebrows. Josie Deckard doesn't *need* anything—at least not from me. She could use a little validation or maybe a call from her absentee father, but she certainly isn't the type to ask for help.

"What's going on?" If she isn't having a melodramatic moment, I might be forced to make good on the threat I made to my mom to leave Palm Springs sooner rather than later.

"There's just a lot of stuff going on," she says. "Leighton is still in the coma, and they've hauled in half of Belle Mère for questioning in the West murder."

"At least they're still looking for suspects," I interject. It doesn't take an advanced degree in forensics and criminology to see that the FBI has already pinned Nathaniel West's murder on his son. It isn't something I want to consider, because I need to believe that Jameson West is innocent. I told him I believed he was, and I did believe it at the time. Also, because he's my boyfriend. Or was my boyfriend. I'm not entirely sure about that now. I rub absently at the still healing cuts covering my forearm. Jameson couldn't have been the one to push Leighton and me through that window, which helps his case with me. If someone wanted to shut us up that badly, they were probably hiding something. However, I'd never gotten the full story from Leighton about who she was protecting. I'd overheard her telling Monroe that she wouldn't tell anyone about *him*. I assumed she was talking about Jameson, but the only thing she managed to tell me was that she was protecting Jonas. Then someone shoved both of us through a plate-glass window. No one can claim the Wests don't throw killer parties.

"It's more than that," Josie interrupts my thoughts. "Do you have your phone?"

I hold it up, and she breathes a heavy sigh that is definitely not one of relief.

"I sent you a message on Instagram," she says.

"Snap a pic of your lunch to share with me? Did you pin some bikini-ready, summer workouts, too?" I ask dryly as I slide past the lock screen on my phone.

In my Instagram messages, I find her note. Clinking on the link she sent, I'm taken to an account I've never seen before. But even though I don't recognize the username—TheDealer— the photos are full of people I know.

"Check out the fifth one down," Josie says in a quiet voice. My eyes flicker back to the computer screen, only to find her own eyes clenched shut. When I reach the photo, it takes a moment for me to see past the blurriness of the picture. It had clearly been taken from some distance. Someone else might not recognize the girl with the wild mop of curls and the petite figure, but I know my best friend when I see her. I don't know the man she's with, though.

"What is this?" I ask in confusion.

"That's Tom," she says. "Or maybe Aaron, I don't remember. It's not important."

"It's important enough that you called me freaking out in the middle of the afternoon to beg me to come home. Who is this guy, Josie?"

"Who do you think?" she asks in measured syllables.

"Oh." Realization dawns on me. Despite how often she ditches me to hook up with random men, I haven't seen her in action until now. "Did you and he ..."

I suddenly wish that I was playing *Madlibs*, so I could finish that sentence with something innocent or benign. *Did you and he save a kitten? Did you and he play miniature golf?* Instead, my mind fills in the blank with visions of rendezvouses that would make E. L. James blush.

"Yes," she answers pointedly, putting me out of my misery.

"How did someone take a picture?" I ask. While Josie might be working through a daddy complex, she's not stupid. A stream of selfies will destroy her life as much as it will this man's. She doesn't take pics of her hook-ups, and she doesn't allow them to either.

"Look closer," she whispers. I scroll through the feed and realize it isn't your typical narcissistic teen feed. No selfies. No documenting every minute detail of a single day. All the pictures on this account are of *other* people—other people we know. Each one is an odd mix of photojournalism and surveillance camera.

"Do you know who took these?" I ask her.

I can't stop looking. It's almost addictive, and I catch myself wondering if I'll make an appearance. The photos are captioned with initials and a location, but nothing else.

"My mom is going to kill me," Josie moans, ignoring my question.

"How is she even going to see these? Your mom's not really social media savvy."

I don't admit that I understand what has her so freaked out. Just the existence of that photo reveals a side of Josie that she keeps under wraps. If this whole feed is full of photos of our Belle Mère cohorts, more than a few people might have already seen it.

"Where did you even find out about this?" I try a different tactic to get the information out of her.

"The account followed me," she says. She pauses as if struggling with whether or not to tell me the next bit. "They're following Monroe, Hugo, and Jameson, too."

"Jameson," I repeat. My heart sinks into my stomach. What photos of him might be on display?

"Are you talking to him yet?" Josie asks.

I shake my head, relieved that there's something more pressing to focus on. "So they're following all of you, but that doesn't mean—"

"Emma," Josie interrupts me. "They're following your account, too."

I put my phone on the desk uncertain I want to unearth my own incriminating moments captured with someone else's camera. "Why would someone do this?"

"To ruin my life," Josie informs me immediately. She's put some thought into this, obviously.

"It's only a photo—" I begin, but she cuts me off.

"That's easy for you to say," Josie shrieks. "If my mom sees these pictures, I'll be enrolled in the Bellevue Girls Academy for the summer session with no parole in sight."

"This isn't *Hamlet*," I stop her, wishing I had a few hundred Xanax on hand. Josie is clearly on the verge of a nervous breakdown while I've been avoiding reality in Palm Springs. "Your mom's not going to send you to a nunnery."

Josie falls backward, disappearing from sight momentarily. The screen goes black, and I squash the panic that rises in my chest. Then she blurs back into focus. I spot her familiar polka dot comforter, and a pillow clutched to her chest. When she finally speaks, her voice is small. "You only see the nice side of my mother."

"At least your mother has a nice side," I grumble. "My mom went nuclear when I told her I was thinking about leaving Palm Springs. It's going to take some serious ego massaging to calm her down if I go." I leave out that she wants me to stay in California permanently. Right now isn't the time to deliver more bad news.

"Look," Josie continues, drawing my attention back to her problem. "My mom is cool, but she obsesses over making sure I have a better life than she had."

"I'm pretty sure that's all parents," I point out. Even though my own have a warped sense of what that actually means, I know their hearts are generally in the right place.

"Let me translate that a little bit better. She's obsessed with me not getting pregnant."

"Can you blame her?" I ask.

She shakes her head and for a moment the screen is filled with her wild, uncontrollable curls. "No, I can't, and that's the problem. I mean, she was only nineteen when I was born, and it seriously set back her dancing career."

"Does she know that you're…" I trail away, glancing out the window to the placid surface of the pool outside. There's no easy way to ask this, because, in truth, even I don't know the answer. When Josie started targeting older guys, I tried to let it roll off my back until she slept with one of our teachers. After that, I asked her to keep the pornographic details to herself. It's easier to take a calculus test if you don't have your best friend's impression of Mr. Barrett's O-face stuck in your head.

"Does she what?" Josie prompts.

"Does she know you've had sex?" The question rushes out of my mouth.

"The list of topics that are off-limits between my mother and I is long and exhaustive, but sex is at the very top of it." Josie presses her fuchsia lips into a thin line, grimacing at the thought. "I'd already be in a *nunnery*, as you put it, if she knew. I mean, I hide my pills in an Altoids tin."

"I guess that answers that question." A million questions tumble through my head. How many men has she had sex with? Why? Is she using condoms? Getting tested? Somehow I manage to swallow them all.

"Does your mom know about you?" Josie asks even though she knows that my sexual rap sheet only has one entry. I was completely honest with her about my first—and only—time. Not that there was much to tell.

"I didn't feel the need to clue her in on my lack-luster first time, especially since I pretty much pretend it never happened," I remind her. Sleeping with Hugo Roth had been a knee-jerk reaction to a terrible situation. I mean, what better way to get back at your cheating boyfriend for having sex in front of half your freshman class than to screw his best friend? I won't be putting that proud achievement on any college applications.

"I don't think my mom would welcome any of the men I've been with in this house."

"Probably not, since they're as old as her boyfriend," I remind her.

Josie smacks her forehead. "Oh, I forgot to tell you. They broke up last week. Men suck."

"How's your mom?" I ask, genuinely concerned.

"She cried for a day. Then she put on some lipstick and met someone new." Josie shrugs but her words are tinged with cynicism. Like mother, like daughter. The Deckards employ a nonchalant attitude toward the "love 'em and leave 'em" philosophy followed by most men in Vegas. The ones who live there full time generally aren't prime cuts of male. Not the single ones, anyway. And the rest of them are tourists whose presence is as fleeting as their luck.

I pick up my phone and stare at the Instagram feed again. It's definitely her, and while whoever's blessed us with this account only identified her by her initials, it hardly feels anonymous. I scroll through the handful of other photos that have been posted. Hugo Roth practically dragging an unconscious girl down the hall. Monroe West, peeking guiltily over a pair of black sunglasses like she knew she was being watched. There's nothing outright incriminating in any of the photos. It's simply the suggestion contained in each one. It wouldn't take a nut job to weave conspiracies in all these pictures. It's clear that's what The Dealer wants his audience to consider. Or her audience, I guess. There's no sexism in stalking.

"Who do you think took these?" I ask.

"If I knew, I'd already have strangled them and stolen their phone," Josie admits.

I study the picture of her for a few more seconds, this time zeroing in on Josie's dress.

"Wait." My mouth goes dry, and I lick my lips. "This is the dress you were wearing the night of..."

But it seems she's already realized that because she gulps and nods. Thumbing back through I find the picture of Hugo with the blonde draped over his shoulder. I can only make out part of his shirt. A *D* and two *E's*.

"STD Free," I mutter to myself as I picture the shirt Hugo wore that night. I'd called it false advertising. Staring at this picture, I stand by that claim. *Conscience-free* would have been a lot more fitting.

"What?" Josie asks in confusion.

"Nothing. It's not important." There's no need to fill her in on the details. "This picture is from that night, too. Why would someone be posting pictures from the night Nathaniel West was murdered?"

I glance up from the phone just as Josie's eyes zero in on me through the screen.

"I have a better question for you," she says. "How many more pictures did they take?"

Chapter 2

AN HOUR LATER, I finally pry myself away from the feed and head into the kitchen. All the paranoia is making me hungry. But a note on the fridge stops me.

Getting a blow out. Back by 1!

I have the house to myself and I've wasted that time stalking some perv's idea of a good time. Sighing, I reach for the fridge door and freeze when I catch a figure reflected in the stainless steel. I spin around and blink a few times as if he might disappear. But he's still there leaning against the doorway. In my defense, he looks too good to be real, but then again, he always has. His wild coppery brown hair is longer than the last time I saw him, falling just over his ears. He rakes it back with one smooth, self-assured motion, but despite the smile playing at his lips, he doesn't greet me. Instead, we stand and stare at each other. Can he sense the line in the sand between us? We'd parted on good terms, at least as good of terms as one can when their boyfriend is being hauled off in handcuffs, but things got a little more complicated since then.

"I'm sorry," I blurt out. "I should have come to visit you."

Lightning flashes in his silver-blue eyes. Without a word, he straightens and strides towards me. Reaching out his hand, he cups the side of my face with his palm, and my eyes close involuntarily. Time didn't dull the electric connection of his touch. Jameson West caught me the first time we met. While we were apart, I questioned that, but now I know I'm gone hook, line, and sinker.

"Don't," he warns me. My eyes flicker open, and I see my questions reflected in his eyes. "Never apologize to me."

I start to pull away, but his hand shifts to grab my chin.

"I should have—" I begin.

"I don't care about any of that," he stops me. "When I heard what happened, I lost it. Are you okay?" He pulls back and grabs my hands, studying the fresh, pink scars marring my skin. "Not being able to come to you nearly drove me crazy."

Is that what happened to me? I wonder. Had being apart from him driven me to insane thoughts? It must have, because here in his presence, all my fears seems ridiculous. His touch erases my doubt, leaving only certainty behind. Whatever happened the night his father was murdered, Jameson isn't guilty of what they think he did. Looking into the depths of his blue eyes, I know he still has secrets, but who doesn't? I have to trust he'll share them with me when the time is right. There are a million things we need to discuss, but being so close to him that I can feel the heat roll off his body, none of them seem to matter.

"This is your home away from home, huh?" he asks, looking past me into the gourmet kitchen that's barely used. There's probably still plastic wrap on the appliances.

"My mother's, mostly. She never really took to Hollywood. It reminded her too much of Vegas." I can't help but wonder what he thinks of the place. My stepfather's sprawling, private estate stretches across the patchy desert, nestling into the foot of the mountains. Someone else might be impressed, but Jameson owns a casino and a mountain home and God knows what else. I really should take the time to Google his real estate holdings.

"Is she home now?"

"She had an appointment in town," I tell him.

He releases a heavy sigh I didn't know he was holding onto. "Thank God."

In one swift movement, his hands slide along my torso, lingering on my hips before they slide further down. Jameson lifts me off my feet and I instinctively wrap my legs around his waist. His face slants towards mine, but he hesitates a fraction of an inch before our lips meet. I can already taste the sweetness of his breath.

"Where's your room?" he murmurs.

It's hard to find words, given the promising situation I've found myself in. My tongue darts out to wet my lower lip, then I jerk my head backward. "Down that hall."

He doesn't need further information. Our mouths crash together as he carries me with the confidence of a man who's walked this corridor his whole life. I barely process him kicking open the door before he deposits me onto my bed.

"I hope I got the right one, Duchess," he says, "Because my patience just ran out."

My fingers clutch my familiar, yellow bedspread, and I nod.

"This is my room," I say softly. "There's a—"

He winks at me. "Give me the tour later."

I gawk as he reaches behind his neck and pulls his t-shirt over his head. Scientists could study the anatomical miracle that are his abs. Perfectly stacked and carved deeply, they narrow to showcase the top of a deep v that I assume continues past the jeans that hang temptingly off his hips. Thousands of tiny butterflies dance in my stomach as he lowers himself with torturous slowness over me.

"Is this okay?" he asks. I bob my head, not trusting my voice. "That is excellent news, because I spent a considerable amount of time imagining what I was going to do to this body."

"What if I'd said no?" I tease, finally finding my voice.

"Then I would have had to persuade you otherwise." His index finger traces across my lower lip, then trails down my chin, along my neck, and further until he pauses in the valley between my breasts.

"Think it would be that easy to convince me?" I breathe, despite the biological urge I have to pant and beg for more.

"I think I could have made you see my side, but I'd be happy to show you exactly how I would have done that."

"I already said yes," I murmur. This time, the smile that's been threatening to appear curves over his face. A strand of hair falls over his eyes and I reach up to push it back.

"That feels good, Duchess," he moans, and I rake my fingernails through his locks. "You've been in my head so long. Feeling you touch me is like waking up from a bad dream."

"I'm right here," I whisper, my voice thick with promise.

He drops lower, nestling his trim waist between my splayed legs. I can feel the rough denim of his jeans through my thin bikini bottom. I wiggle lower, trying to see what else I can discover, but his hands shoot out to keep me in place and I find myself pinned under a very, sexy push-up.

"I promised myself that when I got you in this position, I'd take my time," he says. He bends forward, pressing his lips to the curve of my jaw. "I've waited a long time for this, Duchess."

"Then why are you stopping now?" An impatient hunger blooms within me, and I struggle against the hold he has on my wrists. He laughs softly before he releases them.

"I'm waiting, because I'm not in a hurry. I'm going to make you feel things you've never felt before. I'm going to strip away all the distance time has placed between us, and when I'm done, there will be no doubt that you belong to me," he raises his head and gazes down at me, "if that's okay."

"I guess." I roll my eyes a little at the ridiculousness of that question. My body's been screaming *yes* this whole time. He hardly needs to ask now.

"Where should I start? Your lips?" he muses. He brushes his own over mine, drawing the attention of my nerves upward, if only momentarily.

I moan my approval.

"Or maybe here." He runs his mouth slowly down my neck, settling in the hollow of my collarbone. A slight gasp escapes me, and I grip the comforter tighter. "See? We're just getting started."

It takes all my self-control not to throw my arms around his neck and pull him against me. I'm not entirely sure what stops me, except maybe the fact that I still feel guilty that he's been sitting in a jail cell, or maybe curiosity. I want to see what he can do to me as much as he wants to show me, but before that can happen, I hear the front door slam.

"Shit!" I yelp, pushing him off me. He lands with a thump on the floor. "Put your shirt on."

He reappears not bothering to hide his amusement as he plucks the t-shirt from the floor and tugs it overhead.

"Emma?" Mom's voice echoes through the large open foyer. I glance towards Jameson and brace myself.

"I'm in my room," I call. Standing, I smooth out the bedspread and point to a desk chair. I grab a pair of jeans and a tank top to throw over my bikini.

"You: there," I command in a low voice. He salutes me with his index finger and promptly takes his assigned seat, assuming a saintly position.

"Emma, I was thinking that we should…" The words die on her lips when she steps inside my bedroom. "Um, hello."

Jameson nods in greeting. "It's nice to meet you, Mrs. Von Essen."

She stares at him for a moment longer, frozen in place, then she shakes her head as if to clear it. She smiles warmly. "Vivian."

"Vivian," he repeats, but whatever spell Jameson has cast over her doesn't extend to protect me. Turning in my direction, she shoots me a questioning look.

"Mom," I brace myself for what I'm about to tell her, "This is Jameson West."

"Ah. The famous Mr. West." Her voice piques on his name. She doesn't hold the same animosity toward the Wests that her ex-husband, my father, does, but she's not welcoming him into the family either.

"I'm afraid my reputation does precede me." He stands and extends his hand.

"I've heard a lot about you," she says as she shakes it. I flinch, because if that's true, she hasn't been hearing it from me.

"Mom," I say in warning.

"I have," she says with a shrug.

"Yes." Jameson's eyes dart to mine. "I believe your husband is currently in negotiations with Paramount to do a film based on my father."

"I don't know much about that." It's an obvious lie, but one that most would willingly swallow. If she knows about it, she's kept it from me. Probably to keep the peace this summer.

"Perhaps I'll discuss it with him, then. I'd like to know more." The tension in the room has a greenish tinge that threatens to suffocate each of us, but my mother is oblivious.

"I'm sure he would enjoy that. He has quite a few questions about what happened."

"Don't we all?" Jameson tilts his head. "Maybe he can tell me how the story ends."

Now that our bodies are separated, I can think a little more clearly, which means questions are racing through my head. Apparently, I'm not the only one still trying to figure out what happened. If Jameson doesn't know, the FBI doesn't either. So how did he get out of police custody?

"I didn't know you would be visiting us." Mom walks to the side of the bed and picks up a pillow that's fallen to the floor, no doubt cataloging every wrinkle in my bedspread to use when she interrogates me about him later.

"I wanted to surprise Emma."

"And you did," I jump in. "Maybe we should check out downtown. There's…"

"Will you be staying long?" Mom interjects. Somehow, I've found myself in the middle of a socialite standoff. The weapon of choice? Who can be more polite to the other while slowing bleeding them dry.

"Only as long as it takes to convince Emma to come home."

"And why would she want to do that?" This time she doesn't bother to sugar coat her words.

"Because that's where she belongs."

"In Belle Mère?" Mom asks.

"With me," Jameson corrects.

I step forward, wedging myself between them. "I'm going to take Jameson downtown."

"You'll have to bring him back for dinner," she says, not bothering to tear her eyes away from him.

"Sure," I agree. Grabbing Jameson's hand, I drag him out of the room and toward the front door.

"Your mother is…"

"A piece of work?" I offer. I come to a stop when I spot the white Porsche Carrera with its top down, parked in the circle drive. "Is that yours?"

He grins at me, and this time he's the one leading me away from the house and toward the car.

"If your mom saw my car, she knew she had company," he says. There's an undercurrent of annoyance in his voice.

I wave my hand. "She probably thought it was a spare Porsche that Hans keeps around. I mean, who would notice this?"

"Get in, Duchess," he says, swinging open the door. As I climb into the seat, he bends over and kisses me full on the lips. He circles around the back, and I realize there's so much I have to tell him about what happened that night, about what I heard, and more than anything, he needs to know about the Instagram account before his picture pops up on it.

"Jameson, there are things you need to know," I begin.

He hits the ignition switch. "We'll get to that. First, there's something I need to tell you."

Before I can protest his trumping of my news, he twists in his seat to face me. "They haven't dropped the charges against me."

"Then why are you here?" I ask. "This is a different state." I look around as if police helicopters and a SWAT team might appear over the mountains.

"Don't worry about that."

"Don't worry about that?" I shriek. "Are you out on bail?"

"I am," he confirms coolly.

"Then why did you come here? They just released you."

"To bring you home," he says.

"I want to come back," I tell him, "but maybe my mom is right. Maybe distance is the best thing right now."

"You won't have distance for very long." A cloud passes over the sun as he speaks, momentarily casting us in shadow.

"What does that mean?" I demand.

"They're questioning your alibi."

"My alibi? Don't you mean *your* alibi?"

"*Our* alibi. Emma, they're building a case against both of us."

"Case?" I repeat in confusion. The reality of what he's telling me refuses to sink in or maybe I'm not allowing it to.

"They want to charge us both with my father's murder," he clarifies. Reaching out, he takes my hand. "But I'm not going to let that happen."

"What are we going to do?" I breathe.

Dropping my hand, he takes a pair of silver aviators from the console and slides them on. Then he leans over, bringing his lips to my neck. He drops a soft kiss and a moment later I feel the seat belt snake over my shoulder. "Buckle up, Duchess."

Chapter 3

I SHOULD BE SURPRISED when Jameson pulls into the driveway of a mid-century, mini-mansion—the kind Palm Springs is famous for. I stare him down expectantly, as he waits for the privacy gate to open.

"It's not mine," he assures me.

"Good, because you don't have to buy real estate in every city you visit."

"Believe me, if I was going to buy a house here, Duchess, it'd be next door to you." He pushes his sunglasses down the bridge of his nose and winks at me. "Easier to sneak through your window that way."

And into my panties. "If you can get past Hans' security, go for it, otherwise I suggest walking in through the front door."

He laughs as he hits the gas and speeds into the driveway. Apparently, the Porsche doesn't do slow.

The grounds of the house are as immaculate as the lines characteristic of the time period—sharp and neatly edged. Large, orange blooms cascade over the retaining wall that surrounds the house. It's smaller than my stepfather's place but it gives off a retro-hip vibe that I can't help but admire.

"So whose place is this anyway?" I ask as I climb out of the car. Jameson is at my side instantly, shutting the door behind me.

"A friend's," he says like this is an answer before he throws his arm around my shoulders and leads me toward the front entrance.

Judging from the severe lack of furniture inside, his friend is either really into minimalism or a dude. Inventorying the living room, my suspicions are confirmed. "I'm going to guess your friend is a guy."

"How did you know?"

"Psychic," I say dryly. "One couch, two chairs, every gaming system. A TV that takes up half the wall, and no pictures."

"You're a regular Nancy Drew."

I spin toward him, and trail my index finger along the hard planes of his chest. "Is your friend home?"

He catches my waist and pulls my body against his, dropping his lips to my ear, he whispers, "Does it matter?"

I'm guessing that, according to bro code, friends

don't cock-block friends in their bachelor pads. But as if to undermine my theory, an amused voice interrupts us. "Don't mind me, I like to watch."

I'm so wrapped up in Jameson that it takes a second for the familiarity of the voice to seep into my giddy brain, but when it does, I turn and gawk at the equally familiar face.

"Never fails," Jameson grumbles. "Levi, you have terrible timing."

"I have excellent timing," Levi calls, grabbing an apple from a bowl on the kitchen counter. He takes a bite, and continues to talk as he chews. "That is, according to Michael Bay."

"I wouldn't brag about that, man."

Neither of them seem to remember I'm here. I elbow Jameson in the ribs. There's no point in trying to play it cool now, not when I've been staring like a catatonic fan girl for over a minute.

"Sorry, Duchess." Jameson shifts, and puts one hand possessively on the small of my back. "Emma Southerly meet Levi Rowe."

"I know who he is," I hiss. "What I don't know is what we're doing here."

"Nice to meet you, Em," Levi says, before his movie star white teeth crunch into the apple again. He swallows hard and I follow the slide of his throat. How on earth does he make that look sexy? "I figured Jameson had to have a girl up here if he was coming back to California."

I raise a questioning eyebrow at my boyfriend. "This is the part of the scene where you tell me how you two know each other."

Between the Wests' money, and his sister's brief bid for fame, it shouldn't shock me that he knows Levi Rowe, former teenie bopper heartthrob turned up-and-coming action film star. I'd been safely passed my tween years when he'd been doing his Disney Channel stint, but even though movies about transforming robots aren't my cup of tea, I drooled over his abs like every hot blooded female I know.

As if on cue, Levi steps away from the counter, his unbuttoned linen shirt fluttering open as he strides towards us. *Those abs.* "Jameson brings all his girls here to impress them."

Levi extends his hand, and the two grip each other's forearm as they lean into a masculine hug. Two seconds and a chest bump, I'm beginning to wonder if I stumbled into a frat house by mistake.

"Levi was at Stanford with me," Jameson says. "For what, like two weeks? Turns out his serious college plans were a publicity stunt designed by a movie studio."

"I plan on finishing someday." Levi's lips twitch into the grin that casting directors are willing to pay millions for.

"He plans on getting an honorary diploma," Jameson clarifies.

"Jodie Foster got a doctorate," Levi tells us.

"You're going to have to find a script with less running, and more lines to snag one of those, professor," Jameson advises him.

"I'll have you know my agent sent over a serious part this morning." He glances from Jameson to me, and back again. "And you know, I think I need to go read that now."

"Sounds like a good idea," Jameson agrees.

"Yep," Levi says as he backs down the hall. "I'll be in my room with my headphones on, deep in thought, completely oblivious to the outside world. If you scream for help, or"—he fakes a cough—"any other reason, I won't hear you."

"You're overselling it," Jameson calls after him, but he doesn't miss the opportunity to haul me in the opposite direction. "Come on, Duchess."

I steal a glance over my shoulder as Levi disappears into another room. "We're at Levi Rowe's house."

"Yes," Jameson says.

"You know Levi Rowe."

"Yes."

"Do you introduce all your girlfriends to him?" I ask.

"Not if I can help it."

"Ooh, want to make some wine with those sour grapes? Are you threatened by your friend's brutish masculinity?"

Jameson groans before he laughs. "Are you attracted to my friend's brutish masculinity?"

"Not particularly. Why settle for a movie star when you can have a billionaire?"

"That's my little gold digger," Jameson pauses before a closed door. "I don't introduce my girlfriends to Levi."

"Somebody like to play with your toys?" I ask, but when he turns to stare at me, the light mood vanishes. In the darkness of the corridor, his eyes are shadowy gray and my stomach clenches as they bore into me.

"I don't do girlfriends."

"I thought I was your girlfriend," I breathe.

"You are," he says pointedly.

"Wait." I struggle through the hormones muddling my brain to piece together what he's telling me. "Am I your first girlfriend?"

"I think there was one in fifth grade, Kyla or Kaylee."

"You haven't had a girlfriend since fifth grade?"

"I find girls usually want me for one thing."

"And you're happy to give it to them."

"Money, Duchess," he corrects my assumption. "They want me for money. I want them for sex."

"Let me guess which one of you gets what you want."

He backs me against the door. "Do you know what kind of depraved things people are willing to do if they think there's a pot of gold at the end of the…"

"Blowjob?" I offer dryly. My guess is that Jameson could get most girls in any number of compromising positions even if he were dirt poor. He grins wolfishly, and I wonder if I'm leading myself to the slaughter. "So your friend went to Stanford as a publicity stunt, and you went for…"

"An *education*," he says.

There's a double meaning to that.

"I haven't even taken AP Biology," I whisper. Jameson leans forward, bracing his hands on the door and effectively caging me. I don't want to be just one more sacrificial lamb, but I don't want him to stop either.

"You should know what you're getting into," he says gruffly.

"I'm not as innocent as I look," I protest, but a flutter of panic surges in my chest. Now I'm the one overselling it. Being willing is different than being experienced.

"Don't lie, Duchess." He bends forward and presses his lips to the hollow of my throat.

"I'm not wearing white to my wedding," I remind him.

His laughter tickles across my bare skin. "What? Because some kid sweated on you for thirty seconds?"

"It was more like a minute."

"I stand corrected." His mouth glides along my collarbone. Despite the heady cocktail of frustration and desire swirling inside me, I push against his chest in annoyance.

"If we're going to have a pissing contest, we should do it in the bathroom."

Jameson straightens and meets my eyes. "You have the wrong idea. I like that you're innocent. I like knowing that my hands, my fingers, my lips, my tongue, this"—he presses his hard-on into my soft lower belly and I feel it through the layers of clothing separating us. "get to educate you."

"You sound awfully sure of yourself," I murmur. The kiss he brushes over my lips proves he has a right to be, and a moan escapes me. He wraps an arm around my waist, and I know two things: he's caught me and I don't want to escape. But before the kiss can deepen, he throws open the door behind us. Despite his firm grasp, fear thrills through me in a jolting split second of weight-lessness.

"I won't let you fall," he promises.

Something tells me I already have.

We stumble back toward the bed, fumbling with our clothes, leaving a trail of discarded clothes in our wake until I'm stripped to my bikini and he's down to his boxer briefs. A rare bout of shyness overcomes me, and I'm torn between how much I want to rip off his underwear and my inexperience.

When I finally get up the nerve to slip my fingers past the elastic waistband, he catches my hands and draws them over my head.

"Not so fast," he advises me. "I want you to know exactly what you're getting into."

"I have a pretty good idea," I pant, not bothering to hide my annoyance as my shyness shifts into shamelessness instantly. But Jameson keeps my wrists pinned over my head.

"I got you off in the elevator," he recalls in a lowered voice. "Has any other guy?"

I shake my head, feeling my cheeks flame.

"Then I'm guessing no one has had his mouth on you."

It takes a second for me to realize what he's suggesting. I bite my lower lip, and shake my head again, the flush on my cheeks probably turning to a lovely shade of candy apple red. "Don't be embarrassed, Duchess. I'm going to let go of you now, but I want you to keep your hands up here. Can you do that for me? At least until…"

I nod. I'm not entirely sure what the end of that sentence is, but I have a few ideas what comes after *until*. He kisses downward between my breasts past my navel, sliding his hands along the path until they stop on my hips.

I resist the urge to bury my face in a pillow when he plucks the ties of my bikini bottom. He waits for a moment, as if letting me get used to the idea of what's about to happen, then he draws it slowly down. Suddenly I can't remember if I shaved this morning. Or if I shaved enough. I've seen a Playboy, and I know he has, too. I open my mouth to apologize, but before I can speak, I feel the warm wet plunge of his tongue, nudging its way to the throbbing pulse between my thighs. I arch up, lost for words except for a strangled cry that vibrates from a part of me I didn't know existed. Now I understand what he meant by *until* because my hands fly to his head, grab hold of his hair and push him against me as his tongue works magic. He reaches up and pries my fingers loose. Gripping my wrists, he pins my arms to the bed. He's in charge now. I give in to that reality, allowing my hips to move in unison with his mouth. Dozens of half-formed thoughts flit through my head, prematurely dismissed by a flick or suck, each growing shorter as the pressure builds inside me. Before long, I can't stop myself from bucking against him, and his pleased groan vibrates against my sensitive swollen flesh.

It's enough to send me crashing over the edge. I'm not sure if the screams are in my head, or if I'm bellowing them out loud. All I know is I can find no other word except his name. When I can't take any more, my legs clamp instinctively against his head. Trembles wrack my body and I grip the comforter. I need something to hold on to, because I'm not entirely convinced that I'm not dreaming. He frees himself, then he slides his arms under my torso and gently moves me farther onto the bed. I curl into a fetal position—an instinct they don't tell you about in *Cosmo*—and blink languidly as he climbs in beside me. I reach a trembling hand toward his waist, but he stops me.

"Not right now. That's all I needed." He cradles me to him and presses a kiss to my forehead.

"I…I…" Thoughts are still slow to form.

"Speechless," he notes with satisfaction. "Rest up, Duchess. There's more where that came from."

I BLINK INTO THE SUNLIGHT, then sit straight up, clutching the sheet thrown casually over my lower half. "Oh my god. What time is it?"

Jameson glances up from his phone and smirks. His hair is a tangled mess, and I wonder for a second if it got that way from me trying to pull it out. "Relax. It's just after four."

"Oh my God."

"No, just Jameson."

I flop back down on the bed, sneaking another quick peek at him as I pull the sheet higher. He flips onto his side, and traces the edge of it.

"I have to say that I find your sudden modesty a bit too enticing."

I pull it to my chin. "Mr. West, what big eyes you have."

"Skip to the part where I say, 'The better to eat you with,'" he encourages me, and I slap his shoulder. He falls back beside me, laughing.

"That was ..." I hesitate, before landing on, "Incredible."

"Feel free to write songs and sonnets singing my praises."

"I would, but I don't think it's safe for your head to get any bigger." I turn onto my side, already thinking about round two, until my eyes land on his phone. I stop breathing when I spy the Instagram feed on his screen. "The Dealer should be called The Mood Killer."

"Don't worry about him," Jameson says.

"So it's a him?" Maybe while I slept off the orgasmic coma he put me in, he's found some clues.

"Or her," he adds.

Or maybe not. I scoot up in the bed, shaking my head. "How am I not supposed to worry? That's seriously creepy shit."

"Agreed, but I don't really see the point. Whoever it is needs to be charged with stalking. We should go to the police."

He hasn't been looking closely at all. I reach for his phone, and scroll through the feed. "These two are from the night your father was murdered," I inform him. "I don't know about the rest."

Chapter 4

IF THE DEALER hadn't already put the fear of God in me, facing my mother at the dinner table will. She meets us at the door, offering a simpering smile to Jameson as she directs us to the dining room.

"I hope you like shrimp," she says, but before I can remind her of my aversion to the creepy, ocean spiders, she grabs my elbow and hauls me to the side.

"You're glowing," she accuses.

I half expect her to haul me to the ER to check to see if my virtue is intact. I pull away before she can lose control and make a scene. "Summer love," I say casually before dashing into the dining room.

Hans glances up from his tablet and grunts a greeting. I'm not certain if that's just hello in his native tongue or if we're not worthy of full syllables.

"We have a guest," Mom trills as she enters

behind us. Hans still doesn't bother to look up until she adds, "Jameson West."

That gets his attention and confirms my fears that my stepfather is actually a big enough dick to do a biopic accusing my boyfriend of murder. I guess that really puts the fun in dysfunctional family.

"The infamous Mr. West." Hans's accent is muted by years of being in the US, but it still curls around his words. Between that, his broad shoulders, and what is left of his wispy, blond hair, it's obvious he is an import.

"It's nice to meet you, son." He stands and holds out his hand. The two shake once. I'm not an expert on male greetings but I'd give theirs an eight for formality and a ten for tension. "Hans Von Essen."

"I know who you are, Mr. Von Essen." Jameson doesn't hide the insinuation in his words.

We take our seats as Hans begins to scoff, ignoring Jameson's coldness. Meanwhile, I wish I had a blanket to cope with the chill. "Please, call me Hans."

"I suppose that's fitting." Jameson unfolds his napkin and places it in his lap without bothering to look up from his place setting.

Hans smiles tightly and beckons for the maid to take his tablet. "I'm sorry?"

"To call you Hans. After all, I'm dating your stepdaughter," Jameson offers the alternative explanation, dangling it like a carrot overhead. If Hans goes for it maybe we can spend the evening in awkward silence, making small talk, and escape unscathed.

"I had no idea you two were so close."

Or maybe not.

Hans studies me with interest and I can almost feel the future interrogation now. My love life has never really come up with my stepfather before now. Probably since he had little real interest in me, other than to offer parenting advice to my absentee mother and back up all her paranoid plans for my future. But now I have something he wants, and he's never going to get it out of me. I turn my full attention to the flatware to avoid meeting Hans's gaze while wondering if a butter knife is sharp enough to commit harakiri.

"We're very close," Jameson tells him and I distinctly hear another nail being driven into the coffin that now holds what's left of my stepdad's disinterest. I'm going to miss it. Two parents is bad enough. Now I'll have three at me all the time.

"Oh yes, I have no doubt of that," Hans waves him off dismissively. "I'm afraid I haven't been around as much as I would like. I just wrapped a major film for Paramount and I'm in pre-production on two more."

"They don't want to hear about the business darling," Mom interjects. "People only want to go see the movie, remember?"

"Not at all. What are you working on?" Jameson asks and the question hangs in the air.

The arrival of our salads grants a brief reprieve, but any hope I had of Hans choking on a cucumber slice is dashed when he ignores it entirely. "I'm afraid the projects haven't been announced yet, so I'm not at liberty to share."

"I understand the need for discretion." Jameson tips his head in acknowledgement. But if the butter knife wouldn't be enough for ritualistic suicide, it could definitely cut through the tension in the air.

"I was telling Emma about our thoughts about Los Angeles," Mom pipes up, as if somehow this topic will be less uncomfortable than the first. Jameson's eyes flash from her to me for confirmation.

"And I told her hell to the no," I add.

"Oh, Emma," Hans begins, "there are some very good schools in Los Angeles."

"I'm happy where I'm at," I protest, dropping my salad fork on the table. "Where I *was*."

"I had to beg you to attend Belle Mère Prep," Mom reminds me, "And now suddenly you love it there." I don't miss the none-too-subtle glare she casts at Jameson. "I think you would be more concerned about getting into a good college, then."

"I told you I would take a few classes at UNLV," I say without hope that it will stop her from digging into this topic.

I never intended to make good on that promise.

As far as I'm concerned, I don't need more than a high school diploma to take over the family business. Of course, that was before what happened with my father. Given that the police had used his false claim of assault to hold Jameson for nearly a month, I probably need to reconsider that life plan. "I'm not about to be bullied into becoming a valley girl."

"You don't have to go," Jameson says with an air of authority that makes me cringe. At any other time, I'd find it seriously hot, but considering that we're in the presence of my mother, it only makes me queasy.

"It would be selfish to ask her to miss this opportunity." Hans spears a leaf of lettuce onto his fork, but instead of eating it, he spins it in the light.

"What about the East Coast?" Mom suggests as if we've been discussing my matriculation to Harvard and Yale for years.

"What about it?"

"There are some good schools there," Jameson tosses his opinion into the ring.

I narrow my eyes at him and mouth, *Traitor*.

"Why would I want to go someplace I've never been?" I point out with a shrug.

"You've never been to the East Coast?" Jameson asks. He stares at me like I just announced I'm from a different planet.

"Emma doesn't like to travel," my mother says offhandedly.

"I haven't really gotten the opportunity to." Mom's revisionist history of my travel preferences kills my appetite entirely. I push my plate away. Ilsa appears and whisks it off to the kitchen. I'm like that plate of salad. Suitably filling until Mom grows tired of me. Then it's back to the kitchen for me. She loves to travel, but I haven't been invited on those trips. Over the years, she'd made a few noncommittal statements about taking me here or there, but she's never followed through on any of them. It shouldn't sting as much as it does. But how do you explain to someone that your mother has access to a private jet and you've only seen two states?

"We should go to New York," Jameson suggests, and for a moment it's just the two of us. We gaze at each other across the table as I imagine us frolicking through Central Park. The whole scene is very reminiscent of the opening credits of *Friends*. But the longer he and I stare at each other, the more those scenes start to shift to ones that remind me of *Sex and The City*.

Mom clears her throat and the spell is broken. "Emma is seventeen."

"Thanks for the fact check, Mom," I mutter.

"I don't allow my seventeen-year-old to go halfway across the country without my permission," she continues.

"It's a good thing I'll be eighteen in two weeks then," I jump in.

"Two weeks?" Jameson asks in surprise. "Maybe it will be a birthday trip."

She glowers at him. I want to warn her that her face will freeze like that, but considering the amount of Botox comprising her body, it probably already has.

"I would've thought your people would be a little more thorough."

"Come again?" he asks.

"Someone with your level of wealth has certainly run a background check on my daughter." She folds her manicured hands on the table in challenge.

"Obviously," he admits, "but I didn't memorize it."

"Not something as important as your girlfriend's birthday?"

I don't miss how she makes girlfriend sound like a lot nastier of a word. "Gee, mom. Do you mean slut? Or maybe whore?"

I push my chair from the table, but before I can continue my dramatic exit solo, Jameson stands. "Not everything in this world has to be subject to contracts and legalese and security procedures. I want my relationship with Emma to be real."

"Do you even know what that word means?" she asks him. But despite the coldness of her tone, she shrinks against her seat. Meanwhile Hans watches the entire scene unfolding with interest. I half expect him to yell cut or offer director's notes.

"I'm not hungry," I announce loudly. "Let's go for a drive."

Jameson sucks in a deep breath and squares his shoulders before he gestures towards the door. "After you."

Apologies crowd my lips as we make our way through the hall, but none of them feel adequate.

"Don't even think about apologizing, Duchess," he says as if he can read my mind.

"But they're my parents."

"Only one of them is," he corrects me, "but I can see why you wouldn't want to claim either."

His keys are out of his pocket before we hit the front door, but mom chases after us. "A word, Emma."

It's more than she deserves, but I pause. "Go ahead. I'll be out in a second."

He looks torn as if he's leaving me to fend off a rabid dog on my own while he saves himself. Nothing could be closer to the truth.

"I can handle myself," I assure him. He doesn't need further prodding.

Mom doesn't beat around the bush about why she stopped me. "I don't think it's a good idea for you to see him."

"Really? And I thought you were planning our

wedding." I cross my arms and begin counting down the minute I've given her in my head.

"You have no idea who he is."

"I have a better idea than you do. You didn't even give him a chance."

"I don't have to," she explodes. "I know his family. I know what they're capable of."

"Excuse me," I interrupt her, "but you're the one who was ready to call his Mom a few weeks ago."

"There's a difference between being a West by marriage and being a West by birth," she says.

"Could you be more self-righteous?" I ask her.

"Blood will out, Emma." She speaks as if she's giving me the code key to decipher her cryptic insights.

"If we're done with the riddling portion of the evening, I need to go." I don't wait for her to respond before I turn on my heels and leave my mother—and her opinions—behind.

Chapter 5

"YOUR MOTHER and my father would have gotten along," Jameson informs me as soon as I'm inside the Porsche.

"But who would be the other two Horsemen of the Apocalypse?" I slump into my seat, feeling more than a little sorry for myself.

"Seat belt," he commands. Groaning, I tuck it over my shoulder. It's not like me to forget, not after what happened to my sister, but if my mother can accomplish anything on a daily basis, it's to suck my will to live.

"Where are we going?" I ask him.

"What's the farthest point on the planet from here?"

"I don't know. New Zealand?" Sadly, I don't think this car floats. He revs the engine and peels out of the driveway. Considering how fast he's going, it might just be able to make it across water, but as we reach the main drag of downtown Palm Springs road closure signs greet us. For a brief second, I wonder if my mom now controls the Department of Transportation, too. I wouldn't put it past her to do something that dramatic to stop me from seeing Jameson. But just beyond the white and orange obstacles, a number of tents are set up in the street. People wander, many hand-in-hand with loved ones or children, and music floats through the air toward the car.

Swiveling in my seat, I touch the hand he's using to grip the drive shaft. "Let's do something normal."

"You're going to have to give me some ideas, Duchess. I'm fresh out of normal these days, considering most of our dates end in murder, interrogations, or arrest."

I understand exactly where he's coming from. I tip my head toward the street carnival.

"Really?" he asks incredulously.

"Street food and music and hideous arts and crafts. It's perfect." I unfasten my seat belt and open the car door. "I need normal."

Before he can stop me, I'm halfway to the fair. The tents host various artists and crafters hocking everything from paintings to handmade soaps to any of the hippie paraphernalia necessary for a Californian lifestyle. I peruse them until a familiar pair of hands grabs my hips.

"Come on," he murmurs. "I'm hungry, if that's okay with you."

"Eating is normal," I assure him. But when he heads for a restaurant, I grab his hand and yank him towards the food trucks. "This will be faster."

"What is it?" He stares at the truck as if it is a spaceship.

"What can I get you two?" The man calls from the window.

"How hungry are you?" I ask Jameson. He holds his hands out wide and grins. At least he's going to be a good sport about it, even if dinner doesn't come on bone china. "Four carne asada and four al pastor."

Jameson leans so close to me that I can smell his cologne. My mouth begins to water and I'm not sure if it's from the promise of food or him.

"You forgot to order the side of salmonella," he whispers

"I think they throw that in for free," I mutter.

A few minutes later, and he's devouring his own words with a side of garlic-lime salsa. "Okay, you were right," he grants me, when we toss our empty taco trays in the trash. "I'm converted. Now I'll only order food from trucks."

"I hear there are a lot of food trucks in New York." I throw it out like bait to see if he'll bite.

Instead he spins me around and pulls me close to him. "So you are interested in going?"

"Of course I am." The Empire State Building. Broadway. Fifth Avenue. Why wouldn't I be dying to go?

"Why have you never been to the East Coast?"

"It's complicated and I don't feel like telling sad stories tonight. You know the saying: 'and baby makes three'? Well, according to my parental units, three's a crowd."

"No need to say more, Duchess. I'm going to take you to New York, then London, and maybe Tokyo after that."

"Paris?" I suggest nonchalantly.

"Definitely Paris." Neither of us mention the fact that if he's already in violation of the terms of his bail by being a state away, Europe is out of the question. "I guess it's your birthday, so which one do you want to go to?"

"We don't have to go anywhere," I reassure him. We can dream, but we can't actually revise reality.

"We do." He brushes a sticky strand of hair from my forehead. "They can't cage us."

"They already have," I say softly.

"Then we'll break free."

"Do you really think we can?" I ask. We stand for a moment, clinging to each other despite the oppressive Californian heat. Above us, strings of light twinkle in the twilight like dozens of wishing stars but they can't grant our desires any more than we can.

"What do you want, Duchess?" he asks, reading the silence in my eyes. "The moon, the stars? Say the word, and I'll give them to you."

"You," I whisper. "I only want you."

WHEN WE'VE EXHAUSTED the carnival's delights, we drive to the base of the San Jacinto Mountains. But the farther we get from the lively downtown scene, the quieter we each become until we've left normal behind entirely. Jameson's eyes stare into the distance as he parks the convertible. "Your stepfather's right. It's selfish for me to want you back in Vegas."

"But inevitable," I remind him. If he's right and the police suspect me too, then my return can't be avoided.

"Maybe not," he admits slowly. "Between my lawyers and Hans's lawyers we can probably keep them tied up for a while."

But not forever.

"You shouldn't have to face this alone. If they have questions about what happened that night, *we* need to answer them."

"Emma, we both know we weren't together the entire evening. I left you by the pool. I want you to rescind my alibi."

"But you were with me." Panic boils in my chest bubbling over in a rush of unfamiliar emotions.

"You were with me most of the night. Besides, there were dozens of people there. Anyone could have done it."

"But my fingerprints are all over the scene."

"Yes, because you found the body, and what about my alibi?" I ask. "They found him in his office and that's where we met, so…"

He nods grimly. He might want to believe the investigators are going after me to rattle him, but we both know I had just as much opportunity that evening. Plus, given my family's history with the Wests, nearly as much motive as well.

"You weren't with me the whole night," I repeat, latching on to that fact. If he thinks I'm going to let him play the martyr, he can climb right back off that cross. "Which means *I* was alone, too. If they're going to make you a suspect, they might as well make me one as well. Besides that, you're not going to be able to find who did this by yourself. Not if you're constantly being dragged in for questioning."

"You think they're going to give you an extra recess while I stay in the principal's office?" he points out dryly.

I don't admit that he's right. Not when I need to sound confident about what's at stake. Instead I fall back on classic diversionary tactics. "Why are they so focused on you anyway? You weren't the only one there with motive. I think they're just being lazy."

Judging from how his fingers tighten on the

steering wheel, I've hit a nerve. "It's more than that. Mackey has a vendetta. My lawyers say she wants to see me burn for this."

"Why?"

"I don't have an answer for you, but I'm going to find out the reason she has it in for me."

"Sounds like step one of a plan." Mission accomplished. If he's going after the real murderer, he'll need my help—especially since the cops already think he's guilty. We can't rely on justice being done.

"You should stay," Jameson says as though he can read my mind. There's a firmness in his words that dares me to question him.

"Too bad I'm not the type to take orders," I inform him. "I'm coming back."

"Emma, I thought I needed you to come back with me and even though I miss you, I'll never forgive myself if something happens to you again. We don't know who murdered my father, but we also don't know who pushed you through the glass that night."

"Considering you live in a casino, there's a distinct lack of surveillance cameras in your house."

He blows out a hollow laugh before reaching over to clutch my hand. "Dad called that penthouse his oasis. He said nowhere was safer than at the very top of what he had built. I guess he never considered how far he had to fall.

"Whoever did this came into my home invited because there's no other way they could've gotten past the security team. One of us opened the door to his murderer and let them walk right in."

"It's not your fault," I say in a soft voice. He won't believe it, but he needs to hear it.

"Maybe not," he admits. "My relationship with my dad was complicated, but I owe him justice."

The sun fading swiftly behind the mountains casts a purple haze across the horizon. As the blazing orb disappears from view and the moon takes up its watch, I get out of the car and go to the driver's side. Before he can protest, I climb in and straddle him. Wrapping my arms around his neck, I gaze into his eyes.

"I want to come back with you." I cut him off before he can respond. "I'm pretty damn good at taking care of myself in case you failed to notice."

"I didn't," he says, a wry smile playing at his lips. "Sometimes I think that scares me more than anything."

I raise an eyebrow at this revelation. "Strong women scare you?"

"No," he assures me in a gruff voice as his hands dig into my hips, urging me closer. "I like strong women; I just don't want you to do anything stupid to protect me. Whoever did this, Duchess, isn't going to confess if we find them."

"I don't want them to confess," I say in measured tones. "I want them to pay."

"My father wasn't a good man, but he was my father. I can't help but think that whoever did this probably had a good reason." His words send a chill rippling up my spine. It settles in the roots of my hair until I feel the coldness of it all over.

If the murderer had a reason, what would stop him from piling up more collateral damage? Because in order to get past the lies, we'd have to get closer to the truth—and the person who killed Nathaniel West.

Chapter 6

THE HOUSE IS dark when I tiptoe through the foyer. I refused Jameson's request for me to stay with him at Levi's house. I wouldn't put it past my mother to file a missing person's report. After all, as she recently reminded me, I'm only seventeen. The last thing I need is to get Jameson any more police face time. Given the traumatic dinner earlier, my guess is that mom popped a few Xanax and drifted into the Valley of the Dolls.

But light catches my attention as I make my way to my bedroom. It seeps through a crack in Hans's office door. I hesitate while considering my options. I can go on having a detached relationship with my stepfather or I can call him out on his plans to make a movie based on my boyfriend's life. Neither seem like very appealing options, but I can't go on living under this roof if he plans to use me as a source of information about Jameson.

I creep toward the open door, then knock softly. When there's no answer, I push it open to discover the room is empty. A few scripts are strewn across the desk and curiosity gets the better of me. Wandering over, I sift through the pages and head shots left out until a photo of a familiar face slips out of a file folder marked "Jameson." My heart sinks when I see the notes scribbled on the bottom of the photo of Levi Row. I wonder how much they offered him to sell out his old college buddy. He mentioned that he was about to take on a serious role, and the Academy loves biopics. I stuff him and his traitorous smile back into the folder and sit down not certain what will be worse: if I tell Jameson or if he hears it from *Entertainment Weekly*.

After shuffling through a few more piles, I find a script titled *Wild West*.

Cringe.

I can only hope that's a working title. Flipping through the pages, I discover how thoroughly Hans has researched the situation. He might have played dumb about Jameson being my boyfriend at dinner. But unless he hasn't read his own script, he had no problem agreeing to direct a sex scene that hadn't happened between our characters. With my luck, they'll get some blonde bombshell like Blake Lively for me and I'd get to spend the rest of my life feeling inferior to my fictional counterpart and her fictional sex life. I know better, but I keep reading. It turns out that fictional me is a bit of a slut. My stomach turns over and I rip the page in half, crumple the pieces into balls and throw them into the trash can. If I had matches, the script would already be on fire. Picking up the rest, I dump it on top of the torn pieces. I'm not wasting my time ripping up one-hundred pages sensationalized lies about myself and my boyfriend. Opening the desk drawer, I search for matches. Instead under a pile of office supplies, I find a file marked *Becca*. My hands tremble as I flip it open to find a police report detailing the accident that killed her. I can't bring myself to read about the crash. I lived through it. No amount of clinical objectivity and police lingo could erase those memories. For just a moment, the smell of burnt rubber wafts around me and the rolling sensation in my stomach gets worst. I shake my head until the memories fade. The file doesn't contain much else: an insurance policy, obituary, and the death certificate. I suppose someone had to care enough to keep these things, but it surprises me that it's Hans. I trace her name. That's all she is now, words on paper. Becca is a collection of memories and facts-date of birth, time of death, mother, father. The tip of my index finger stops on the word typed under name of father.

Unknown.

Why would Becca's death certificate list her father as unknown? Mom and Dad had been divorced before the accident but that didn't mean he wasn't her father. It didn't make any sense unless...

I continue to stare at it as if it will start to make sense or forge a new meaning, but I'm no closer to making sense out of it when Hans clears his throat from the doorway. I slam the folder shut hurriedly.

"Can I help you, Emma?" His large body fills the door frame and I shake my head. "I see you've been reading my script."

"You've got a few details wrong," I inform him in a cold voice. I shove Becca's file underneath the ones containing head shots before I lounge back in his office chair and grip the arms until my hands hurt.

"I'd be more than happy to consult with you and Jameson on the project."

"I doubt he's interested in helping make a movie that claims he's guilty of murdering his father."

"Don't you know that fame is the new jury of your peers?"

"Jameson isn't on trial for his father's murder." My protest sounds weak, even to me.

"He will be," Hans assures me. "Let me help him."

"And you making a movie saying he did it is going to get him off. Pardon me, but I call bullshit." Hans doesn't balk like my mother at my use of curse words. Instead, he walks inside the office and takes the seat across from me.

"He's young, good looking. He had to have a reason to do it. If the audience likes him it won't matter if he's guilty."

"He didn't do it," I repeat myself, but Hans either doesn't hear me or doesn't care.

"Perhaps there's a tragic story. His father hit him or molested him."

"Oh my God. Do you hear yourself?" I stand up knocking a few pieces of paper to the floor. "You can't just make things up."

"Of course I can. I work in Hollywood," Hans chuckles derisively.

"Does mom know that you put a sex scene featuring her daughter in this movie?"

"She already knows that you're his alibi," he says meaningfully.

"That doesn't mean we have sex."

"You're really so winningly innocent." He pauses and looks me up and down. "It's going to be hard to cast you. I need an actress that can play naive but fuckable."

"I need to go throw up now." My hand flies to cover my mouth as I try to keep the churning at bay. But as I round the corner of the desk, he stands and steps in front of me.

"Aren't you going to ask me about the other thing?"

I swallow and try to channel some of that winning innocence. "I don't know what you're talking about."

"It's part of the charm," he says, "how terrible of a liar you are."

I try to push past him but he holds me in place. "Ask me."

There's a threat running through he's words now.

"Why do you have that file on Becca?" My voice is small, because I don't want to know the answer. Not while I'm still trying to wrap my head around that one word: unknown. I knew my sister. She'd been there every day of my life. I'd been born into a world that was already hers and nothing has felt right since she left it. The idea that her existence—and my life—are comprised of lies is too much to bear.

"Becca was very special to me," Hans says. His grip on my arm loosens but he doesn't let me go.

"I know." As much as I don't want to fill in that unknown with his name, it can't be helped.

"You do?" he asks in surprise.

"I saw…" What exactly did I see? The certificate itself proves nothing, which means I'm about to take a big leap without a safety net.

"Saw what, Emma?" he demands. He presses his palms flat on the desk and leans in to catch my eye. "How long have you known?"

"A few minutes," I answer in confusion.

He bristles as if my lack of long-term study of the subject affronts him. "You never suspected?"

"Why would I suspect that?"

"She didn't tell you?"

"She knew?" If Becca had known that we had different fathers, she'd taken that secret to the grave. If that's true, she'd been my best friend and I hadn't known her at all.

"You gathered the truth from that stack of papers. You're very intuitive." His fingers slide up my bare arm. It takes a second to process the meaning behind his touch but my body backs away before my mind catches up.

"What the hell do you think you're doing?"

"I miss your sister," he says. "You look like her, you know?"

My mouth goes dry. "We were sisters."

"You remind me of your sister. You're as beautiful as she was, maybe even prettier." He moves toward me and I scramble to think of a way out. "I used to screw her on that desk."

"You were her father." The accusation spills out of me and stops him in his tracks.

"What?"

"That's the secret. The one that you were hiding." Even as I say it, the truth forms with startling clarity, but now I want it to be something that's as benign as my mother lying about an old fling and then marrying him later. Because the new picture in my head can't be erased.

"I'm afraid only he and your mother know who her father is. Although I suspect your dad knows as well. Your sister was ambitious," he continues, and I want to scream at him to stop talking about her because I don't want his memories of her. I want mine. I want to believe I was her best friend. I want to believe that the furthest she ever got was with a Topher Drake at his Halloween party her junior year. "I loved your sister."

"No, you didn't," I correct him.

"That's not fair. I love you both."

"I didn't ask for your love." I rush toward the other end of the desk but my foot catches on the rug and I tumble down into the chair.

"Becca had dreams," Hans tells me, "and dreams take money."

"Do you even know the difference between the truth and lies anymore?" I start to push myself up but he leans over me.

"That pretty little mouth of yours will get you into trouble." His hot breath, still stinking of tonight's shrimp entree, makes me gag. "I'm a reasonable man. For instance, take this sex scene that's bothering you. Maybe you didn't sleep with him." He stands up and his fingers find his belt buckle.

NO. NO. NO.

It's the only word I can process but I can't get it out of my mouth. My heart pounds against my rib cage like a trapped animal trying to break free. I want to run, but I'm frozen in place, afraid that the slightest movement will encourage my predator to lunge.

"Maybe you gave him head," he suggests. "I can see you doing that."

I struggle to find my voice and when I do questions flood from me."Is this how it was with you two? You forced her into doing what you wanted?"

"Becca liked to please me. Maybe you should be a little more like your sister." He unbuttons his trousers. "Why don't you show me what happened that night? Show me how I need to rewrite the scene."

Sensing my opportunity, I find the courage to stand up. I'm careful to push the chair back to give myself more room. Hans mistakes that for acquiescence.

"That's good," he coaxes. His hands reach to rest on my shoulders so that he can gently urge me to my knees.

"I think the whole scene needs a rewrite," I tell him before I swiftly introduce his groin to my kneecap. He's down long enough for me to get out of the room and into the hall. I pull my cell phone out of my pocket and dial 911. When he stumbles to the doorway and starts to lunge, I hold up the screen. "One more step and all they hear is me yelling for help."

"You're nothing like your sister." He spits at my feet.

"No, I guess I'm not."

IN MY ROOM, I lock the door and shove a few things in a bag, makeup, a couple T-shirts, my swimsuit, and grab my laptop. There's a 10% chance I can convince my mom to mail me the rest, but I can't tell her what happened, so she'll probably hold it hostage until I'm brave enough to show up at her door again.

You remind me of your sister. Hans words swim in my head until I'm dizzy trying to forget them. It's not like the first time I've been compared to Becca, but this was different. I resist the urge to walk into the shower, fully clothed, and turn the water to the melt-your-skin off setting. Nothing can wash this away.

I send two text messages, the first to Jameson. I didn't bother to type more than *SOS*. Not while my fingers are still shaking. To Josie, I managed to get out two words: *Coming home.*

Now I just have to wait and not go crazy, which feels impossible. I want to get away from here and pretend this never happened.

Instead, I stare in the mirror for a moment

trying to find Becca hiding in my green eyes. I'm having a hard time picturing her. I can recall all the facts: strawberry blonde hair instead of my sandy blonde, more freckles, particularly on her nose. She never tanned if she could help it. I have all the pieces of the puzzle but it's getting harder to figure out how to put them together. That's the real cost of grief. People you lose slowly slip away until they're nothing more than a list of memories you can't recall.

"Get yourself together," I command the girl in the mirror, but she looks scared and small. I don't want to hug her, though, I want to slap her. Instead I wander back into my bedroom. I could pack another suitcase, but somehow I don't want any of these things anymore, not if they were bought with Hans's money. My eyes fall on a framed picture from last summer. Becca and I are laughing as mom and Hans try to look serious in the background. We need a family picture, mom had said. This was as close as we'd gotten. Now it's all we have. I grab it off the desk and fling it to the ground.

You break it, you buy it, right?

I'd been bought with private school tuition, a new car, and my mother's happiness. What had he bought her with?

Bending down, I pick up the frame, shaking the rest of the broken glass free so that I can pluck the photo out. It should be comforting to see my sister staring back at me given literally only moments ago I couldn't conjure up her face, but it's the exact opposite. I've looked at this picture every day this summer, but today Becca seems different. Is her smile forced? Is she really laughing? Did he assault her and she covered up for him, thinking no one would believe her, not even me? Hans wants me to believe the worst, but what if he's telling the truth? What happened between Hans and Becca?

"It's really inconvenient that you're dead," I say to the photo. A rush of hot tears aches in my throat, but I swallow against the pain.

Digging through my desk drawers, I find another photo of the two of us, shot at closer range. We're hugging on a beach in La Jolla. Becca's blue eyes stare back at me.

The only blue eyes in the family. Mom's voice floats to my mind. I'd need a biology text book to be positive but, if memory serves, it's pretty rare for my father's brown eyes and my mother's green eyes to produce a blue-eyed child. Recessive genes, my ass. The shrill ring of my phone startles me, and I toss the picture back on my dresser.

"I can't get through the gate," Jameson says, and I detect a note of panic in his voice.

"I'll open it but meet me at the front door as soon as you can."

"What the hell is going on, Duchess?"

"Just meet me."

Shouldering my duffle bag, I brace myself as I unlock my door but Hans isn't waiting for me. Running down the hall, I'm a few steps from the front entrance when Jameson's headlights glare through the window. A sob of relief bursts out of me.

"Where on earth are you going?" my mother calls from the top of the stairs.

"Home," I tell her.

"I did not give you permission."

I ignore her and open the door. "I'm not staying in this house a minute longer."

"You seem to be under the mistaken impression that you make the rules around here—" my mother begins.

"You're under the mistaken impression that it's safe for me here." I'm not even sure she can hear me past the sobs that choke my words. I can't hold any of it back. Not anymore.

Even in the dark house, I see her face pale. She takes a few stairs down but stops again. "What does that mean?"

"Ask your husband."

Chapter 7

I DON'T HAVE to tell Jameson to drive fast. He's off the Von Essen property in record time. I don't ask questions when he heads away from the city. Jameson could take me anywhere as long as it was far away from that twisted dollhouse.

Moonlight casts stark shadows over Palm Springs. Tonight it looks black and white and every shade of gray in between. It's a city of ghosts. No place for me.

Jameson pulls into the private airfield just beyond the public airport.

"What about the car?" I ask as he collects our bags from the back seat.

"What about it?"

A one-time use Porsche? Jameson West is so out of my league.

"You have a pilot available to pick you up at

midnight?" I stare at the crew refueling the small private jet.

"That surprises you?"

"No." I shrug trying to look nonchalant and failing miserably. "I mean, the rest of us are stuck search Travelocity and taking red-eyes."

"I think this qualifies as a red-eye Duchess."

A man in a pressed uniform approaches us and Jameson hands off our bags. "Are you jealous of my private jet?"

"My mom has one." Which isn't exactly true. Hans's studio does, and there isn't a shot in hell that I'll be going aboard Hans's flight deck anytime soon.

"Then we're two peas in a private jet pod."

"Been waiting your whole life for another girl with a private jet?"

He knits his fingers through mine. "Private jets, questionable childhoods, we were made for each other."

I rest my head on his shoulder thankful that he's not pressing me for more information about why we're waiting at a private airstrip in the middle of the night. I might have used up my allotment of normal for the day, but I'm grateful that he's here cracking jokes. It's strange that the circumstances surrounding our relationship are so dramatic, given how easy it is to be with him.

"They're ready for us," he announces. I follow

him on board and immediately remember that there's West money and what's left for everyone else on the planet. Apparently private jets can be divided by class—and Jameson's is clearly platinum. The seats are upholstered in buttery leather and champagne-gold subtly accents each surface.

"Do you want to get some rest?" he asks hitching a finger toward an open door. I peek inside and find a small but adequate bedroom that might have come in handy if I felt like facing the inevitable onslaught of nightmares about tonight's events. Instead, I shake my head. I figure there's two ways to deal with my trauma: self-inflicted insomnia, or dreams Freddy Krueger wouldn't dare enter.

"I don't feel like sleeping." I don't have to say anything else. Jameson takes the hint and we settle into two leather seats facing one another. A stewardess, who must have trained to be a ninja in another life, appears instantly beside us.

"May I bring you something to drink Mr. West?"

"A whiskey and soda. Laura, allow me to introduce Ms. Emma Southerly."

She turns her warm bubble gum pink smile on me. "What can I bring you Ms. Southerly?"

I refrain from ordering all the booze in the world because that certainly isn't going to help me stay awake. "Can I have some coffee?"

Caffeine is not only a safe bet, but a necessity at this hour.

"Absolutely, I just put a fresh pot on," she chirps. She scurries out of the private compartment and I wonder how many pots of coffee she's had. No one should be this alert at this time of night.

Looking back to Jameson, I find him studying me, but he doesn't speak. The silence stretches through the delivery of our drinks and take-off. When Laura excuses herself after we've been in the air for a while, he unbuckles and comes to my side. Kneeling next to me, he takes my hand. "I need you to tell me what happened."

"Nothing," I lie because I don't want to tell him. Repeating what happened between Hans and I means facing the information he gave me, not just what he tried to do. I know how to protect myself against pervs, what self-respecting Vegas girl doesn't, but nothing can change what he told me.

"Emma," Jameson prompts when I'm quiet for a few more minutes. "Did Hans hurt you?"

"Yes," I stammer. "No! Not like you're thinking."

But then again, hadn't he?

"What did he do to you?" His voice is danger-ously low, quiet with a rage that anything I tell him will only fan into uncontrollable fury.

"Nothing happened," I say in a rush, choosing to cling to obliviousness.

"Jesus Christ, Emma." His grip on my hand tightens. "You're scaring the shit out of me."

"He tried." I leave it at that.

"Did he...touch you?" Jameson asks in a strangled voice.

"He tried," I repeat, "but I kneed him in the balls."

"That piece of shit. Why didn't you tell me?"

"Because I knew you'd react this way, and the last thing I need is another member of my family charging you with assault."

"That man isn't your family."

He doesn't have to tell me that twice.

"Do you want to talk about what happened?"

I shake my head quickly. Maybe when I've had a chance to process the things Hans claimed happened between him and Becca, I'll need to talk about it. For now, I'm more than happy to pretend that it's all lies. I need to pretend, because missing my sister is hard enough without worrying about whether or not I knew her at all. My thoughts flash to Hans unbuckling his belt and I swallow against a bit of bile that rises in my throat.

I got away, but I almost hadn't. The idea that he might have forced me to do that to him when I never have before only makes it worse.

Without thinking, I jump to my feet. Jameson drops back to his heels and stares at me.

"Stand up," I order him.

"Duchess?" But he complies, and I kiss him hard on the lips resting my palms against the ridges of his abdomen. The contact gives me the courage I need to slide one of my hands lower, past the loose waistline of his jeans to the warm, rock-hard bulge that seems as eager for this as I am. But as soon as my fingers sweep over it he pulls back, circling my wrist with his hand.

"Duchess, I don't think it's a good idea."

My eyes narrow in annoyance. "I've already had one guy try to tell me what to do with my body tonight. How about you let me make my own decisions?"

It's logic he can't argue with, but before he tries, I drop down on one knee and then the other, sliding both my hands to the button of his jeans. I unfasten it, then I slide the zipper down until I can draw them off his narrow hips. I might be the one on my knees, but I feel powerful. My newfound courage surges through me, and I tug his boxer briefs down to his ankles.

It's not the first time I've touched a dick, but it's the most face time I've ever had with one. Until this moment, the whole process seemed pretty simple: take off pants, put in mouth, suck. Now that I'm getting a chance to study Jameson West's most impressive asset—and that's saying something—I wonder if I'm in over my head.

It's different than I remember. Strained, veins

bluish with trapped blood, and long—so long that I am wondering how it will fit in my mouth.

And, for that matter, anywhere else.

"Duchess," he whispers in a hoarse voice. "You don't have to." He rakes his hand through my hair gently, reminding me exactly why I want to do this. I wet my lips with my tongue then I lean forward and lick. In the back of my head something Josie told me once comes to mind and I giggle.

Treat it like an ice cream cone.

"You're going to give me a complex," he warns. "Is it funny?"

I bite my lower lip and peer up at him. "No," I breathe. "It's delicious."

"Then feel free to have another taste," he says with a smirk. I take him up on the offer, running my tongue up and down and swirling it over the broad tip until I'm brave enough to lower my mouth over him.

The hand on top of my hair fists as a low growl of pleasure rumbles from his chest. "That's it, Duchess," he encourages me. "Oh fuck, just like that."

I bob my mouth up and down, my confidence boosted by the dirty words spilling from his mouth. "Your hand," he grunts. "Use your hand."

I grip it firmly, and he reaches down guiding my fingers along his length in unison with the rhythm of my mouth.

"Fuck, I'm going to come," he warns me in a strained voice, but when he nudges my head to push me away I hollow my cheeks and suck harder until a strange heat floods the back of my throat. It takes a little effort to gulp it down, but I manage with a couple gags. Apparently, I won't be going pro at blow jobs anytime soon.

He hauls me up by the elbow, his eyes half masked with pleasure and kisses me deeply. When we break apart he takes a deep breath. "Oh my God, that was ..."

"Not God," I stop him, "Just Emma Southerly."

Chapter 8

IT'S JUST past two in the morning when we land in Vegas. We're far enough away from the neon signs of the Strip, that the only light is from the blanket of stars overhead. I spot Josie leaning against her beat-up junker. Judging from the shorts, tank top, and vacant expression, she's still half asleep. Jameson raises an eyebrow when he spots her. "I could give you a ride home."

I force a tight smile. "I'm not going home."

Realization flashes in Jameson's eyes. With everything else that has been going on, it's easy to forget that home is not my happy place currently. "You could stay with me, and we wouldn't get into trouble at all."

I shake my head, and this time the grin on my face is real. The thought at staying at Jameson's house turns me into a puddle of melted jelly, and that's exactly why it's a bad idea. The thought of waking up next to Jameson is tempting. But I doubt we'd ever go to bed, or at least to sleep.

"My parents are already really pissed at me," I remind him, and given the events of tonight, I doubt that's about to change.

"Screw your parents. You'll be eighteen soon."

"Yes, I will," I confirm with a peck on his lips. "Call me crazy, but that's a little young to be living with my boyfriend."

"Okay, you're crazy," he teases, hooking his fingers in the loops of my jeans. "I think we're old souls."

"That might be true, but according to our driver's licenses, I'm a minor and you're already in enough trouble."

"I've never seen either of those facts on my license." He tilts his head in acknowledgement of that fact, but I can tell he's still not buying what I'm selling. That's okay, he doesn't have to. I'm the only one who has to live with my decision. "You sure I can't convince you otherwise?"

"I'll visit," I promise him. "You're going to be sick of me, Jameson West."

"I could never be sick of you."

"Wanna bet?" Part of me hopes that's true, but even with my questionable background in relationships, I don't think that's how it works.

"We won't know until we try."

"Spoken like a guy trying to get into my pants."

He leans forward, each of his breaths tickling my ear as he whispers, "I've already been there, Duchess. I just miss my happy place."

"Are you saying my vagina is your happy place?"

"Baby, it's my personal Disney World."

Josie coughs loudly behind us, and we startle apart. "Now that you two have ruined my childhood"—she pauses to yawn—"can we get going? Some of us need our beauty sleep."

I throw my arms around her and squeeze. Some people go home. But for me, some people are home. But before I can join her in the car, Jameson catches me around the waist. "Are you sure I can't convince you otherwise?"

"Well, no," I say a bit too forcefully. He drops his hold on me. "I mean, no. It's not a good idea."

He glances from me to Josie, then he kisses my cheek. "I'll call you tomorrow, Duchess."

"When?" I asked, as he starts to back away. It's a little sad that I want to plan my entire day around him. Sometimes a girl has to give in to her cravings. He shrugs, looking like a definition of the word cocky, as he stuffs his hands into his jeans pockets. "Depends on when I get up and around. I have a hard time getting up out of bed."

"Do you?" I ask.

"Sure you don't want to come over and see what I mean?" he offers.

I roll my eyes. Then I turn and loop my arm with my best friend's.

"Why are you passing up that invitation?" she hisses under her breath.

"Trust me, the invitation is open."

I MAY HAVE WOKEN Josie up, but her mom is just getting off her shift at the MGM Grand. She throws open the door to the tiny matchbox the Deckards call home as soon as we reach the front stoop. Her face is freshly washed, her dark skin glistening with moisturizer, and her hair is pulled into a tight knot at the top of her head. She's also doing her best impression of a pissed-off lioness.

"What the hell do you ..." she stops as soon as she sees me. "Oh my God, darling."

Marion throws her arms around my shoulders and gives me into the perfect hug. When you see moms and daughters in movies and on TV, this is what it looks like. At least that's the closest approximation to maternal affection I've ever known. Vivian Von Essen isn't known for warm hugs.

"I didn't know you were back."

"I just got in," I told her. "Josie gave me a ride."

"Emma's just going to crash with us, if that's okay."

"Your daddy knows?" Marion asks. But even as she begins her interrogation, she hauls me inside. A few minutes later, and she's got omelettes cooking on the stovetop. "Okay, now that I don't have a knife in hand, spill. Why are you staying at our house?"

"If it's not okay," I begin, but she holds up a hand, showcasing long, teal nails that undoubtedly match her costume for the latest show she's dancing in.

"You're always welcome in this house. But I saw how you hesitated when I asked about your daddy."

"We had a fight before the accident," I admit to her, "and things got ugly. Then Mom wanted me in Palm Springs… "

As much as I love Marion Deckard, I don't want to go in to more details about the shit sandwich life's been feeding me of late.

"He's probably worried about you."

"Yeah, well…" I press my fingertips into the tines of the fork she sat out on the bar. "Trust me, he doesn't expect me to come home."

"Do you want to talk about it?" she asks.

I shake my head. I'm just about all talked out. The talking never seems to cease. First everyone wanted me to talk about my parents' divorce. How was I feeling? Who did I want to live with? Then mom got remarried and I had to talk about her new husband. Was I excited? Did I like him? Where did I want to live *again*? At the time, I didn't have anything to say about him. That's certainly changed. But nothing was worse than when they started pleading with me to talk about Becca. *Share what happened that night. Share your favorite memories of her. Share how you're feeling.* No one wants to know when all you feel is numb.

At least when the police came around and started asking me to talk about Nathaniel West's murder they wanted facts, not emotions. They didn't need to know if I was sad or happy or scared. They just wanted a play by play. After tonight and the accident last month, there are going to be a lot more things for people to ask me about. I need to gather strength for the oncoming inquisition.

Marion shoves the carton of eggs into the overly crowded refrigerator and closes the door. Leaning against it, she stares me down. "Do you feel safe there?" One bad choice couldn't change a lifetime of feeling at home, right? But when I open my mouth, all that comes out is a small "no."

"You stay here as long as you need." She doesn't press me for further information. There's no threatening to call the police. No after-school special drill about talking with adults you trust. She's known too many men in this town not to read between the lines.

Josie reappears from the bathroom and takes the barstool next to mine. "That smells good." She peeks past her mother to the omelette pan.

"You better make one yourself if you want one."

"Oh, I see, Emma gets spoiled," she teases as she heads to the fridge. Pretty soon she's standing next to her mom, tending her own pan. Marion begins to hum, and Josie jumps in, singing the lyrics of what sounds suspiciously like a Taylor Swift song.

Marion whirls around and drops the omelette on my plate with the skilled ease of someone who lives primarily on eggs. I've never said no to her signature dish. Then again, I've never been offered anything else.

Turning around, she bumps her hip against her daughter's, and the two continue their duet while I take small bites. Between the buttery smell permeating the kitchen and the easy atmosphere, my appetite returns.

I try to help with dishes, but she shoos me away. Josie excuses herself to bed, but I linger in the small living room, staring at an old photo of me with Josie and Becca. Marion had taken it at some little carnival that had popped up in a grocery store parking lot. We had just come off the spinning cups, and we were still giggling and falling all over each other out of dizziness. One simple snap of the lens and she'd managed to capture pure happiness.

"I miss her every day," Marion says quietly.

I nod, my mouth too dry to agree with her. Somehow given Hans' revelation, I miss her even more. She feels farther from me than ever. Time is supposed to heal grief, and instead, it seems to keep finding new ways to open up the wound.

"Did she ever talk to you about a boy?" Boy is definitely the wrong word, but saying anything else might give away the situation. I don't give a crap what happens to Hans, long may he burn in hell, but I do care about how people remember my sister, especially about how I remember her.

"I wish." Marion moves beside me and shakes her head sadly. She wraps an arm around my shoulders and pulls me in closely. "But getting a Southerly girl to talk is a bit of a challenge."

She might be right, but no one wants to hear what I have to tell.

"I met her boyfriend." My stomach clenches on the white lie. "Or at least some guy who claims he'd…you know."

Marion pulls a few inches back and bites her lip guiltily. "I did take her to the doctor to get on birth control."

"Oh." I want something to hold on to. I need something to hold on to. I should be used to grasping at straws and holding on to whatever shred of happiness reality tosses my way. I don't know how to find my footing with this. Becca definitely wasn't with any guys here. It doesn't prove Hans' story, but it supports it.

"Was the boy nice?" Marion asks.

For a moment, I forget the lie I fed her, but even when I process what she's asking me, I can't stop myself from telling her the truth.

"No."

Chapter 9

I SEE Becca in my dreams. It's her face. When she laughs, it's her voice. She glances towards me with a stranger's blue eyes, but she doesn't see me. She walks past me and through an unmarked door. When I follow behind her the room is dark and empty. I sit down and cry. There are a million questions I want to ask her, but even in the dream I know she's gone and that I'll never receive the answers I want.

Before, not knowing bugged me; now it hurts. Each second in the dark room seems longer than the last and the sadness takes over until the sobs roll powerfully through my body. Then there's a hand on my shoulder. I blink against the tears, trying to see in the darkness, certain Becca has come back for me, but as my vision returns, it's Josie's face that greets me.

"Are you okay?" she whispers, her voice groggy with her own dreams. "You were crying in your sleep."

I swipe a few tears lingering on my eyelids. "I'm fine."

"Do you want to talk about it?" Josie scoots lower in the bed until we're face to face. I'm not sure what to tell her. I still don't know how what I've learned about Becca will affect my memory of her, but I want to keep the information to myself. Josie shouldn't have to shoulder the burden of looking at one of her best friends differently. After all, the living can make amends, but the dead can never change.

"I was dreaming about Becca," I admit to her. "I don't remember much else."

"Was it hard to be in Palm Springs without her?" Josie asks. It's an obvious question and one she's nearly asked me a dozen times. I've known her long enough that I can tell when she's chickening out on addressing a topic.

I gulp against the sharp stab of ache her question produces. If she only knew how much Palm Springs had changed everything. "Yeah. It was weird."

"Is that why you left?"

Whatever has been holding her back from drilling me this summer is obviously no longer an issue. I can't expect to avoid questions when I up and run away in the middle of the night and land on my best friend's doorstep. It's a tad bit comforting to know that she's still here and willing to force the uncomfortable topics. But I don't want to talk about what happened in Palm Springs.

"I think I missed home," I say instead.

"Does home have an adorable dimple when he smirks?" Josie guesses and just like that the mood lightens, shifting subtly like the sky outside her window that's slowly changing from inky black to the purplish hues of dawn.

"Yes." It's one truth I don't have to hide. It's not as if I can camouflage my feelings for him. "Jameson isn't the only thing I missed about Vegas, but he's definitely top three."

She clucks her tongue in reproach. "I'd put him higher than that."

"Are you checking out my boyfriend?" I smack her shoulder playfully.

"Girl, you can't miss that ass."

"No, you cannot."

Josie can brag on my boyfriend all day long. The thought of being jealous where she's concerned is so ridiculous, I nearly laugh. Not only do I know he's not her type, but I also trust her with my life. That means I definitely trust her with my boyfriend.

"Does he look that good naked?" she asks in a hushed voice like her mom might be standing with her ear pressed to her bedroom door eavesdropping.

I bite my lip suddenly feeling a little self-aware even as my mind flashes to memories of his chest and arms, of his legs and *everywhere* else. "I haven't exactly seen him naked."

"I cannot believe you aren't tapping that," she squeals. "There's picky and then there's prude."

"And nothing in between," I note dryly. Trust Josie to stick to the black and white ends of the sex spectrum. "We've screwed around and I'm pretty sure I've seen most of him."

"Details?" She insists, clutching her pillow like she's settling in for a bed time story.

I give her the laundry list of what we have done together, which might be short but I still think it's impressive. When I finish, she feigns wiping drool from her mouth. "So you're going to have sex with him, right?"

"I guess," I hedge.

"Oh my god, what is stopping you? Is it that stupid checklist of yours?"

What is stopping me? Jameson has proven to be nothing short of perfect. Well, he might be a little controlling, but it's not like I'll put up with that shit so it hardly matters. "No," I shake my head. "I'm pretty sure he's hit all the requirements."

She grabs my hand and squeezes it so tightly that she nearly breaks a finger. "Even love?"

Fuck a duck, that's a big one. Even though I've never written down all the requirements I had for my second time, love has always been at the very top.

"It's a simple question," she prompts me.

Am I in love with Jameson West? I haven't felt like I've been falling for him so much as hurtling with him for the last few weeks. But doesn't the fact that I didn't hesitate when she asked if he met *all* of the requirements mean something? The problem is neither of us have actually said it. We've tossed the term around, trying it on to see how it sounds, but we haven't gotten to those three little words.

"You're in love with him," Josie says it for me.

"I don't know, I mean..." I stammer as I try to think of a way out of this subject. But as the first sliver of sunlight appears on the horizon, everything becomes illuminated. "Yeah, I am."

Josie, for her part, is practically seizing in the bed with excitement. The realization just makes me feel nauseated.

"What if he doesn't love me?" I ask her in a quiet voice.

She abandons her mattress jig and props herself up on an elbow, wagging her finger at me. "I've seen how that boy looks at you. He's been waiting at the love party for you to show up for a long time."

"He hasn't said it," I tell her.

"Who cares if he says he loves you? He shows he loves you. It's a lot easier for a guy to say *I love you* than to prove he means it. Trust me."

And I have to because of the two of us, she's the one who knows.

Neither of us can fall back asleep so we get dressed quietly. I borrow a light cotton t-shirt and a pair of cut-offs from her when I realize my bags are full of unmatched outfits. At least I grabbed underwear.

"Maybe we should swing by your house?" she suggests. "You could grab some stuff."

I bite the inside of my cheek and look for an excuse but she's right. Josie and I aren't exactly built the same way, which means our sartorial overlap is limited. Going home means I might run into my dad, though. The last time I saw my father was a bit of jumble. I have a faint memory of him visiting me in the hospital after the accident, but I was too drugged out at the time for it to count. Going back home, even to retrieve my belongings, might send the wrong message. After what Hans did, Dad looks better in comparison. But it doesn't undo what he did.

"Okay, spill," she demands when I remain silent. "What happened between you and your dad?"

I thought my fight with him was the low point of that evening until things got much worse. I'd been in no shape to tell Josie about it and from the time I wasn't on a perpetual dose of opioids, I'd wanted to forget that it had ever happened.

But you can't crash in your friend's bed indefinitely without giving up the goods. "He found out about Jameson and me."

"Oh, shit." Josie freezes and gives me her full attention leaving one eyebrow unlined. "I'm guessing he didn't take that well. Did he kick you out?"

I shake my head. That would have been far less complicated. "No, he tried to start a fight with Jameson and I got in the way."

"What are you saying?" Josie asks slowly. She's starting to put the pieces together, but she's still going to make me say it.

"He hit me—punched me to be precise." The nonchalant attitude I'm going for is completely undermined by the way my voice cracks when I say it aloud.

"Oh my god, I'm going to kill him." Her tone rises to an octave somewhere between shrill and ear splitting.

I wave my hands frantically before she gets too loud and wakes up her mom. "He was aiming for Jameson. I jumped in front of it."

"That doesn't make it right, Em."

"Agreed." She doesn't have to tell me that twice. "But it's also not abuse, so don't even think about calling him in."

"You mean like he did to your boyfriend? Did Jameson pummel him before or after he hit you?"

"After." Admitting it is cringe worthy.

"I'm sorry but I have to say this; what a piece of crap."

"I think he was trying to protect me," I say, dredging up one of the many theories I'd overanalyzed for the better part of the last month.

"By hitting you? Don't play that game, Emma."

"No, by turning Jameson in. He honestly thinks the Wests are dangerous."

"Someone did kill the patriarch," Josie points out.

"You make it sound Shakespearean." I take my phone off the charger and toss it into my bag.

"Shakespeare knew a thing or two about fucked up families," she reminds me.

"Mr. Hunter would be so proud of you right now," I tell her, thinking about the overeager English teacher at Belle Mère Prep.

Josie leans into the mirror to finish her other eyebrow. "Speaking of Hunter, what do you think of him?"

"As an educator?" I say with meaning.

"In general," she says bypassing awkward and going straight for uncomfortable. At least, she's abandoning the topic of my dad.

"I think you already do well enough in that subject."

She flashes me a wide grin in the mirror, and I'm reminded of one of the other reasons that Belle

Mère feels like home. "Oh, honey. I don't do it for the grades."

WHEN WE REACH MY HOUSE, I do a double take when I spot a white Mercedes, still sleek with factory wax, in the driveway. "Does he have company?"

"If he does, she has good taste," Josie says appreciatively. She pulls in next to it and eye fucks the car for a few seconds. I can't blame her. Her Civic isn't much to look at, but it is dependable. Two characteristics that mean nothing to a teenager.

Meanwhile, I stare at the house. The blinds are drawn, as usual. Pawnography, my dad's pawn shop off the Strip, doesn't open for a few more hours, which means he's probably home. I haven't had the heart to check in with Jerry, his manager at the store, to see if Dad's been coming in.

"So, he's here." Leave Josie to face my conundrum head on.

"Yep." Facing things isn't my strong suit.

We lapse into silence and she finally makes a suggestion. "We can come back later."

"There's a pretty good possibility he'll be here later, too." I unbuckle my seat belt and take a deep, steadying breath. There's also a good possibility that he's passed out from whatever he drank the night before. If so, I can probably get in and out before he knows I'm here.

"Wait, if he has company, do you really want to go in there? They could be…you know…"

She rolls her hips for emphasis.

I roll my eyes, "Gross."

"Just saying. I can go in if you want."

But I've made my decision. "No, I can do this."

When I reach the front door, I find it's unlocked. I'll be lucky if the whole place hasn't been robbed in my absence. But everything is in its place and there's no evidence of squatters. The only difference is that Dad isn't on the couch. I consider peeking into his bedroom, but if Josie's right and he has someone over, that's the last thing I want to see. I already have step-daddy issues thanks to Hans, there's no need to further scar me.

My room is exactly how I left it, unmade bed and all. Most of my luggage is in Palm Springs, so I gather whatever bags I can and shove the contents of my closet inside.

"Emma?"

I jump, discovering my dad holding onto the doorframe. I can't tell if sleep or booze weighs down his eyelids.

"You're home," he says, but I shake my head vehemently. I don't want to give him false hope. I'm not back to save him.

"No, I'm just here to get some stuff."

"Your mom called," he continues ignoring my denial. "She said you took off but she didn't say why. That's the car she got you in the driveway."

That's a better explanation for the phantom luxury vehicle's presence than I could have hoped for. Then I remember she bought it with Hans' money. Maybe later, I'll take it to the desert and torch it. "Where are the keys?"

"On your dresser." He points to the fob. "It's been waiting for you. I was tempted to take it out for a spin, but I was hoping you'd come home."

"I didn't," I repeat. "I'm staying with Josie, I just need some clothes."

"Look, Emma I think it would be better if you stayed here."

I abandon the packing and glare at him. "Right now what you think doesn't matter. I feel safer at the Deckards."

My words are a verbal slap across his face. He recoils, shame flitting over his features before he looks at the floor. "I know you don't believe this but it was an accident."

"Yeah, I accidentally got in the way of the fist you intended for Jameson." I don't miss how he winces when I say his name. "Then you accidentally filed the police report against him for assault. I could have done the same to you, but I didn't."

I zip my old gym bag shut and throw it over my shoulder. The rest of my stuff is shoved into a couple of reusable grocery bags I found at the bottom of my closet. There's a lifetime of memories in this room that can't be packed away.

But maybe it's time to leave them behind.

"You're still a minor," he says finally.

"Is that the only card parents have?" I ask him, recalling how my mom said the same thing that last night in Palm Springs. "Because I won't be a minor in a few days. So if you want to force me to stay here until I turn eighteen, go ahead. But when I do turn eighteen, I'll walk out that door and you'll never see me again."

"I don't want that," he begins.

"No, I didn't think so," I continue, not allowing him to interrupt my diatribe. "I need to come back on my own if I decide to come back at all."

"I want to make this right." There's a vulnerability in his voice that I've never heard from my father. I guess dads aren't supposed to show their weaknesses. He'd never been able to hide his. I'd just never been one of them before.

"Then give it time," I advise him.

Sliding past him, I head down the hallway.

"Are you still seeing him?" he calls after me.

I stop and turn to face him. "Yes."

"Just to upset me?"

I shake my head. It's not the first time in my life I feel sorry for my father. What can make a person stop believing in other people? "No. I'm still seeing him because I love him."

I drop that bombshell and then I walk away, leaving him to figure out how to cope with the damage.

Chapter 10

IT TAKES an embarrassing amount of time for me to realize that there is no key or ignition in this car. If I wanted to torch it before, now I'm planning on driving straight to get some gasoline for the bonfire. It's Josie who finally figures it out.

"Try that," she says, pointing to a button that reads on/off.

I press the brake pedal and then I hit the button. The engine purrs to life.

"This car is so sexy." Josie runs her fingers over the leather armrest. If I'm not careful she's going to orgasm on the spot.

"I hate it," I say through clenched teeth.

"Because it's from your mom or do you have problems with luxury cars in general?"

"You want it?" I dangle the key fob between us.

Josie flicks the bottom of it, then sighs. "This is

yours, girl. I'll keep looking until I find a sugar daddy who'll buy me my own."

I know one who would. I nearly gag at the thought.

"Enjoy it, Emma," she advises me. "It's been a shit year and it's just a car. Who cares where it came from?"

Maybe she has a point. I decide to christen the car *Pain and Suffering*. It's a fitting name. If I'm going to cover the cost of years of therapy by myself, I guess I can accept the car.

"Care to go on a joyride?" I offer.

"I'd love to but I promised my mom that I would drive her to work this summer so she didn't have to figure out parking."

"Isn't it a bit early for her to be going in?" I glance at the digital clock on the dash. I realize it's already 8:30 in the morning, but Vegas doesn't exactly run on traditional work schedules.

"She has a fitting." Josie groans as she pets the sleek console between us. "I really wish I could stay and play. I have a feeling this is the beginning of a beautiful friendship," she murmurs lustfully.

"Get out of my car." I shove her playfully. "Before you leave a stain on the passenger's seat. I need to run a few errands, anyway. I'll catch up with you later."

"Okay," she agrees, then she leans over and air kisses my cheeks.

"What was that for?" Trust Josie to make me

laugh when I'm trying to be pissed off about something.

"You're a sophisticated woman now," she says. "You drive a Mercedes."

"That doesn't make me European."

"Whatever you say, darling." She blows me a kiss before she climbs into her car.

Considering that I hadn't planned on coming back to Belle Mère so soon, there's more than a few things I need to tackle on my to-do list. I know I should triage the items—decide which is most important and start there— but there's one activity I can't put off any longer.

Belle Pointe is a smaller hospital, not the trauma center that I'd been brought to after the accident at Jameson's penthouse. After a few days, I'd been released from that hospital into my mother's care. Leighton hadn't been so lucky. Sometime in the last month, they moved her from Las Vegas General to the cushy private institution.

Undoubtedly, it's closer to her parents but it has to cost twice as much. She still hasn't woken up, so I'm not sure she appreciates the upgrade. I don't know what to expect when I stop at the front desk. "I'd like to visit a patient."

"Fill out the chart." The nurse doesn't bother to look up from the paperwork she's sorting. I search for a pen for a few seconds before she reaches out and plucks one out of a ceramic planter. The top of the pen has a flower glued to it.

"Cute." I take it from her.

"You'd be surprised how many pens wander off." She shrugs and returns to her work. Not only is this place super swanky, judging from how hard it is to tell the waiting area apart from a lobby of a 4-star hotel, but it also conducts social experiments on important topics like pen stealing. As if they couldn't afford to buy more pens given how much a place like this costs.

I write down Leighton's name, then mine, and the time before I hand the clipboard back.

She checks it, then eyes me for a second. "Are you a family member?"

"Do I have to be?" I ask, unwilling to commit to an actual answer.

"You just look a little like her."

I almost tell her that I was the other girl in the accident—the one who walked away with a few bad cuts and some stitches—but it's not a fact I want to boast about.

"How is she doing?" I ask.

"Not my floor," the nurse admits. "You can ask the attending when you get up there. She's in room 321."

Despite the hefty price tag this place comes with, they don't bother with much security. I head

toward the bank of elevators. Stepping inside, I spot
Jonas just as the sliding doors shut. I guess I'm not
the only one back in town. I hadn't seen him since
the accident, but Josie, who somehow knows the
geographical location of half of the school, has kept
me up to date on his family's travels for the summer.
I consider hitting the button to open the doors,
instead I hit the one for the 3rd floor.

It seems impossible to go from wanting to talk to
someone every day to having nothing left to say to
them. Somehow Jonas and I accomplished that.
Although, I'm pretty certain he perfected it years
ago. I hung on to a relationship that had been over
for an embarrassingly long time. Chasing after him
now seems like a step in the wrong direction.

The third floor is relatively quiet. The woman at
the nurse's station doesn't look up as I pass or when
I double back to head in the right direction.

I stop in the doorway, realizing far too late that
Leighton's room isn't empty. Hugo leans into view
before I can make a quiet exit.

"Pawn Star," he says affectionately. Hugo Roth
has the amazing ability to sound like he's compli-
menting you and insulting you at the same time. A
stranger might have found his greeting friendly, but
I know that its intended effect is to keep me in my
place, beneath him on the social, financial, and
sexual scales. He's one of the original Housers, the
group of students at Belle Mère Prep, who make it

their mission to squash as many people beneath them as possible.

"What are you doing here?" I ask him as I move hesitantly into the room. I don't mean to come off so accusatory, but he's always brought out the bitch in me.

"Someone needs to visit her," he says in a flat voice.

I don't push him on it because I can hear how much he hates this question in his reply. "I just got back in town," I explain to him. "My mom didn't want me to come back until I was fully recovered."

Hugo looks me up and down then turns away, and stares at Leighton. Something about him looks lost until he finally speaks. "You look fine."

"I guess I was the lucky one," I murmur in a low voice. Seeing Leighton connected to a half-dozen machines that monitor her heart rate, breathing, pulse, and a number of other things I don't recognize is a pretty harsh reminder that I was fortunate to walk away that night. In the giant hospital bed, she looks small. Her skin is too pale, and they've chopped off some of her blonde hair on one side where stitches still pucker her scalp. On the other, her hair still brushes her shoulder.

"What do her doctors say?" I ask the question and then realize how stupid it is. Why would Hugo know that?

To my surprise, he answers, "There's brain function although it's not as strong as they'd like. Really, it's just a waiting game."

"What are we waiting on?" I ask him.

"Whether or not she wakes up." His fingers twitch and it takes a second for me to realize that he nearly reached out for her hand. I back up a few steps, feeling the need to give them space. I should ask him about The Dealer and try to get the scoop on the rumors floating about Belle Mère. He's always had a finger on the pulse of what's going on in our tiny enclave. Instead I say, "I'll leave you two alone."

"You don't have to," he says. "She's not much of a conversationalist."

I tug my purse strap higher up my shoulder. Right now, I don't feel very social either. I search for a topic knowing that half the things on my mind, I shouldn't even bring up. "I saw Jonas," I blurt out.

"That must have been exciting for you," he says in a snarky voice, which I ignore.

"Just as I was coming up. He was leaving."

"You thought you saw Jonas." Hugo corrects me. "He's in Indiana, or Illinois, or Omaha visiting his grandmother."

"You just named like half the country," I say. There's no doubt in my mind that I spotted Jonas. Considering that Hugo can't even remember where his best friend is supposed to be, it hardly matters.

"He's somewhere in the middle then."

If 'by the middle' he means downstairs, then he's right, but I don't push him on the subject.

"What are your plans for the rest of vacation?" I ask when I can't come up with anything else to say to him.

Hugo groans loudly, running a hand through his spiky blond hair. "I think I might learn how to do macramé. What are yours?"

"The same." I don't miss the resentment in his voice. I roll my eyes recalling that when it comes to Hugo Roth, you need full body condom, because he's such a dick. "I guess I should go."

I should be the one in that bed. Not her. I back toward the doorway and when my foot hits the outside hall, Hugo calls after me, "Emma, thanks for stopping by."

I blink a couple of times trying to process that he just showed appreciation for something I did. "You're welcome."

I make it a few steps towards the elevator before I turn around and creep back to Leighton's room. Hugo has his hand over hers as he whispers to her. I can't make out what he's saying, but it's enough to make me comprehend that miracles are possible because Hugo Roth has a heart.

I'm inside the elevator when a far less welcome realization hits me. I do look like Leighton. It isn't that it *could* be me in that bed, I conclude with sickening certainty.

It was supposed to be me.

Chapter 11

A BELL over the door tinkles as I walk inside the shop. Nostalgia surges through me, not just because the store is full of crap but because I spent most of my life calling it home. There were times when I slept on a cot in the back with Becca. I'd been working off the clock since I could count in order to fly under child labor law regulations. I used to consider myself an integral part of keeping this place functioning, now I know I was just a Band-Aid. I can't spend my whole life being the glue that holds my dad together, and this is the first place I need to let go of if I'm going to send him that message.

Jerry pauses from rearranging a display of Civil War era pistols and glances up to greet his customer. His joy is instantaneous when he realizes it's me. I'll bet he's been waiting a long time for his lunch break. He hurries out from behind the counter to greet me, pushing his floppy hair out of his eyes.

"I was wondering when you would be coming back." He goes for a hug and I let him, patting him awkwardly on the shoulder as he squeezes. "This place isn't the same without you."

I'm pretty certain that what he means is paychecks are irregular, deposits aren't making it to the bank on time and he's stuck here all hours of the day. But I'll take the compliment.

"I just popped by to grab something." There's no way to soften the blow, so I don't try.

The smile falls from his face. "Oh. I thought you were home to help for the summer."

"My Mom doesn't want me working at the shop, because of...the accident," I lie.

Jerry lets out a long whistle. "Do you think that's wise? I don't know how we're going to keep this place running."

We're not.

"I'm sure dad will make sure everything stays on track." I sidle past him towards the cash register. He watches me with interest, but he doesn't try to stop me. I'm not here for money. I doubt there's any to speak of, anyway.

"We both know that isn't true, Emma. He can't keep this place up without you."

Apparently Jerry managed to grow some balls

while I was away in Palm Springs. I've always pegged him as more of a 'take it and like it' type. The kind of guy who spends his nights in one of those scuzzy little hole in the walls getting spanked by a woman in leather. I open a drawer and dig until I find the business card I threw in here a couple weeks ago, sliding it into the back pocket of my cutoffs, and slide the drawer closed. Jerry deserves better than to be lied to, especially after all the years he's put into this store. "You're probably right, but I can't spend the rest of my life holding him up."

"You shouldn't have to," he says in a soft voice. "You're too young...and pretty," he tacks on awkwardly.

I give him a small smile, hoping it doesn't encourage the crush he's been nursing on me for the last few months. Jerry's sweet, but I can't stay behind to help him out. I head toward the door, finally ready to leave this place behind for good. I pause and drink it in one last time.

The jerseys signed by long-retired athletes, guitars played by former rock stars, guns used in war, and knickknacks collected by children who grew into adults who no longer needed their treasures. The whole place is like a warning to let things go. Here, time doesn't seem to flow. It just stops, and if you're not careful, you can get trapped. I turn, and push up on my tiptoes to give Jerry a kiss on the cheek. "You shouldn't get stuck here, either," I advise him.

"Somebody has to keep it running." He scratches his head, following my gaze around the large, open store, and I can see that he's trapped here.

"Yeah, my dad has to keep it running," I remind him. "These aren't your burdens, and they're not your treasures."

I leave it at that, calling out over my shoulder, one, last time. "See you around, Jerry."

"See you, Emma."

Before I get in the Mercedes, I pull the business card from my back pocket and stare at it for a moment.

Dominic Chamber.

He came to me with a forged Babe Ruth baseball card. In the end, he left with the fake and gave me this. I hadn't known I'd need to use it. Now I know why I saved it, but, asking for help—drawing attention to a problem I'm not sure exists—makes me feel sick.

I shove the card in my glove box. Maybe I'll let it marinate there for a few days until I know what I want to do. As I pull out of the parking lot of Pawnography, I know it's the last time I'll visit.

It's bittersweet. I thought this place was my future—a ball and chain, that I'd have to drag with me my whole life. Maybe things never would be the same between my Dad and I, but I have to admit that his actions finally set me free.

"Ugh, Emma," I say to myself, gagging a bit. "Can you sound sappier?"

Reaching into my purse, I search for a pair of sunglasses to ward off the midday glare coming through my windshield.

There's only one person I want to see right now. I'm about to call him when I notice a maroon Monte Carlo behind me. It sticks out, because the same Monte Carlo was parked at the back of Pawnography. You tend to notice the other car in an empty parking lot. Against my better judgement, I slide on my phone and hit Instagram. It looks like The Dealer's been busy today. On the top of his feed, there's a photo of Josie, carrying a Weckman's drugstore bag full of toilet paper. I try to scroll down while keeping my eyes primarily on the road, but, there's nothing new of me...yet.

The Monte Carlo's windows are tinted, so I can't get a good look inside and the driver is staying far enough back that I can't see any other details. Flipping on my turn signal, I decide to test my theory by maneuvering across a couple lanes of traffic at a suicidal speed to take the closest exit. Sure enough, Mr. Monte Carlo follows me.

I've got The Dealer in my sights, or at least my rear-view. Now I just have to figure out what to do with him. So far, this asshole has been content to channel his inner-paparazzo, but what happens if he realizes I know he's following me? The thought chills my blood, and I hit auto dial.

Jameson answers after one ring. "Morning, Duchess."

"It's nearly afternoon," I inform him.

"So it is," he says with a yawn. For a second, I'm distracted by the thought of him stretching his magnificent arms over his head, wearing nothing but a sheet.

"I have a problem." I have to remember to get to the point.

"What's wrong?" The languid sexiness is gone from his tone, replaced by urgency.

"I'm pretty sure someone's following me. I think, maybe, it's The Dealer." I glance in the mirror to check if he's still there. He is.

"Well, stay on the phone and come to me."

"No. I'm trying to think of a way to trap him. Like, maybe I'll pull into a store and wait, and when he goes to follow me in—"

"Come straight to my house," Jameson cuts me off before I can rattle off the rest of my half-hatched plan.

"I'm not driving all the way up to Mount Charleston."

"You're driving? Whose car?"

My hands tighten on the steering wheel. "Jameson! Where can I go? I'm not going to Mount Charleston."

"Our place in Belle Mère," Jameson corrects me.

"How many freaking houses do you have in this city?" I snap, panic getting the better of me. So much for calm and calculating. Apparently I'm going straight to uber-bitch.

But he ignores my attitude and begins to rattle off directions.

"I'm not going to remember any of that."

"Then just stay on the phone and tell me where you are." It takes me seconds to find the cross streets, but when I do, he heaves a sigh of relief. "Okay, I want you to take your next left."

He navigates me to his house with saint-like patience. The Monte Carlo follows me the whole way.

"Your gate's closed," I tell him when I turn into his drive and see the wrought iron monolith blocking me from safety.

"I just opened it." As if on cue, the panels begin to slide to the side. I wait just long enough to be certain the Mercedes can fit through before I zoom forward. Any other time, I might waste precious seconds by admiring his house, but the Wests' real estate portfolio is the last thing on my mind.

Jameson is waiting on the front drive, wearing nothing but a pair of jeans. His feet are bare, his abs are on display, and judging from the tousled mess of coppery hair sticking in every direction, he really had been in bed. All I can think about is having those strong arms wrapped tightly around me. I put the car in park, not even bothering to turn off the engine, and run to him. Burying my face in his chest I breathe in his scent: soap and the remnants of yesterday's cologne mixed with a little sweat, like he'd been tossing and turning in his sleep.

He tips my chin up with his index finger. "Promise me you won't go around acting like live bait?"

"I just thought—" I start, but he cuts me off.

"It's not safe, Emma, and I need you to stay safe."

"Yeah, I'm your alibi," I mutter, trying to pull away.

Jameson holds me tighter. "You know that's not why I need you to stay safe, Duchess."

"I'm sorry ..." But the apology dies on my lips when the Monte Carlo barrels down the driveway.

"You didn't shut the gate," I yell at Jameson.

"I need you to stay calm," he says.

I wrench away from him, instantly realizing that there is more to this situation than he's letting on. "What did you do?"

"I need you to stay safe," he repeats himself.

"What did you do, Jameson?" I demand. The driver of the Monte Carlo climbs out of the car and walks towards us. Pausing at my car, he leans in and turns off the engine.

That's weird behavior for a psycho.

I expected The Dealer to be someone we know —someone who has a stake in our secrets—but I've never seen this man before, and I know I'd remember him. The guy makes The Rock look like a weakling. He could probably eat The Rock for breakfast. His neck is wider than his head, bulging with veins that pulsate down to his broad shoulders and inhumanly large arms. If someone told me he was smuggling pythons around those biceps, I'd believe it.

"This is Maddox," Jameson informs me. "He's a former Navy Seal."

"And my new stalker," I add.

"And your new bodyguard," Jameson corrects.

I whip around to face Maddox, not realizing how much closer he's come to me. I have to crane my neck so that I can see his face when I tell him, "Thanks, Maddox. Nice to meet you. We won't be needing your services."

Maddox glances at Jameson, who gives a condescending tilt of his head, as if to say *you're dismissed for now* before he grabs my hand and drags me inside.

"I do not need a bodyguard," I say through gritted teeth. "The thought of someone following me around night and day is enough to drive me crazy."

"I disagree with you," Jameson says.

"That doesn't matter. I didn't give you permission to hire someone to follow me around."

"No, you didn't. But I cleared it with your mother."

"You spoke to my mother?" I begin to pace, needing to put distance between us, even if it's only a few steps. I guess he's siding with her on the whole *Emma is a minor, we can do whatever we want to her* issue.

"I assumed that you'd fight me on this."

"And you didn't think I'd fight my mom on it?" I ask. If that's true, then Jameson West doesn't know me half as well as he thinks he does.

"This is about your safety. I don't want to control you, I just need to know that you're safe."

"You keep using that word. I don't think you know what it means, because I am safe. The accident was just that: *an accident*."

It's obvious that he's been preparing for this reaction, because he doesn't blink. "Hans and your mother had security on you the whole time that you were in Palm Springs."

"What?" This I didn't expect. "I barely left the house."

"They sat outside the house, and when you did leave, they followed you."

How on earth had I missed that? "You all should

win awards for paranoia. I'm going to get the lot of you tinfoil hats for Christmas."

"It's not paranoia, Duchess. Someone pushed you through that window. I can't be with you all the time." His tone isn't pleading, it's firm. This has been decided for me. "When you decided to leave Palm Springs, I reached out to your mother because I wanted my man on you."

"I don't want any man on me," I tell him, shoving him in the chest. "Especially not you at the moment."

A growl of frustration vibrates through him and he moves forward, backing me toward a wall. "They would have sent Hans' men," he informs me, "and I don't want that creep to know that you so much as ate breakfast this morning."

"That doesn't give you the right to have me followed."

"It's a precaution. Nothing more." When I go to argue, he smashes his mouth against mine, kissing me until I'm senseless. My rage seeps away. It's an effective way to the end the conversation.

My fingers run along the stacked plane of his abs, vibrating on each one. Now I know where they got the term *washboard*. I break away, panting heavily, my lips still brushing over his. "This conversation isn't over."

"I'm not stupid, Duchess." He licks my lower lip in invitation.

"You're very stupid," I moan. "With your stupid mouth and your stupid body."

"That's it, baby. Try to stay mad." He rocks against me, encouraging me to focus on a very different, but equally intense, range of emotions. "You're so cute when you're angry."

"I'm about to be goddamn gorgeous!" But I can't keep my lips away from him. Jameson answers my kiss with a groan as he lifts me off my feet. My thighs make contact with the heat of his bare skin and I give in to the wild woman trying to claw her way out.

I am mad at him. A message which he probably isn't getting since I'm wrapped around him like a pretzel. I snake my arms around his torso and dig my fingernails into his back. He responds by pressing me against the wall.

"Let it out, Duchess," he urges me. "Show me how pretty you are when you hate me."

Oh god, I wish I hated him. It would make it so much easier to walk out that door and take control of my own life.

"I hate you," I murmur against his mouth and he sucks my words away with a kiss, plunging his tongue deeply into my mouth. Since he's not going to let me verbally get my point across, I rake my nails down his back.

He winces audibly before whispering, "I told you I like it."

Rough? I'll give him that. When he goes to kiss me again, I bite down on his lip until iron floods over my tongue. He pulls back and runs his tongue over his injured lip. "If you aren't careful, I'm not going to be able to stop."

"Stop what?" I demand breathlessly.

He answers with a thrust that I feel through two layers of denim.

"Did I ask you to stop?" I ask.

"Be very careful with what you say now, Duchess," he warns me, "unless you want to find yourself naked in my bed."

"Maybe that's exactly what I want."

"You hate me," he reminds me.

I love you. The words trip over my tongue but I swallow them away. Now isn't the time to reward his behavior with affection.

"Goddammit, Jameson, take me to bed."

"No way," he says with a grin. "Not angry. At least, not for the first time."

I can't help but like the idea that there'll be a second time or a third. I don't think I could ever get enough of him, and if he keeps acting like this, we'll have plenty of angry sex in our future.

But there's an ache building inside me that can't be ignored, so I decide to change my tactics. "Don't you want to take me to bed?"

"Fight fair," he advises me. "I can't handle it when you pout."

I stick out my lower lip, realizing I have all the ammunition I need to get my way. I circle my hips, rubbing against him. There's more than one way to get a rise out of him. "Please?"

"Christ." He grabs my hips and forces me to stop. "I want to stay in control."

"And I want you to lose control," I whisper.

"Is that what this is about? A power struggle?" He nuzzles my neck before nipping the curve of my shoulder. "Because you hold all the cards, Duchess."

I stop pouting and revel in his admission.

"You look pleased with yourself," he notes.

I press my heels into his back, forcing him to crush his body harder against mine. "I hold the cards?"

"Yes," he mutters.

"Then take me to bed," I order him.

Chapter 12

.

HE KISSES me as he swiftly maneuvers our tangled bodies across the foyer toward the stairs, but before he can carry me to my requested destination, a familiar voice shrieks.

Jameson stops and we break apart, our eyes still locked together. "We have company."

"So it seems," I mutter. "What's a girl have to do to get some?"

Jameson chuckles softly as he extricates his body from mine, placing me safely on my feet.

"Jameson, dear," his mother calls, "please put a shirt on. It's nice to see you again, Emma."

"You, too, Mrs. West." I don't bother to pretend that I'm happy to see Monroe with her. The two of them are laden with shopping bags.

"Would you like some help?" Jameson offers,

stepping away from me. I already miss the feel of his skin on mine.

Trust love to turn me into a wide-eyed, helpless sad sack.

"Shirt," she repeats. I have to smother a giggle at the frustration that flits across his face, but Jameson nods and dashes up the stairs.

I stand there for a minute, trying to decide where to go. Following him seems like a bad idea, because unless I'm mistaken, his mom just put the kibosh on our afternoon sexscapades. Instead I wander past the foyer until I find myself in the kitchen.

"Oh, hell," Monroe mutters when she spots me. "Mom, the maid forgot to take the trash out."

"I forgot. I got you a present," I tell her. Then, I give her my middle finger.

"Classy."

"I learned it from you," I say with a fake sob.

She twirls around, her stick-straight, blonde hair whipping over her shoulders as she drops her bags on the kitchen island. Jameson reappears with his mother on his heels. This time he's wearing a shirt, and grabs my hand, bringing it to his lips for a quick kiss. Evelyn studies him for a second before giving him an approving smile. "That's better."

He winks at me and heads towards the fridge, kissing his mom on the cheek as he goes. He pulls out a box of pizza but before he can open it, his mother bats his hand away.

"I can't believe you're going to eat that."

"I'm hungry," he protests, but he tosses the box in the trash.

She ruffles his hair in affection. "Did you just get up?"

Monroe glances at me and smirks. "Something's kept him in bed, obviously."

Jameson doesn't miss a beat, immediately picking up on what his sister is implying. He comes over and throws an arm around my shoulders. "Emma just got here. Unlike some, she's a lady."

"I don't know what you're insinuating." Monroe shrugs as she studies her manicure. I know exactly what he's saying, but I keep that to myself. "I just call it like I see it."

As much as I despise Monroe, I like Jameson's mother. There's no need to make things any more awkward. I'm pretty certain her walking in on our make-out session covers that. Evelyn West has not only perfected the ability to look polished at any given time, but also the ability to ignore it when her children squabble.

"Emma, would you like something to eat?" she asks me as she pulls a vegetable tray out of the Sub-Zero and places it on the counter.

I shake my head. My nerves are still raw from trying to evade my own bodyguard this morning

and I'm on edge after the fight that I've left unfin-
ished with Jameson.

"Probably for the best," Monroe says. "It looks
like you were eating well in Palm Springs."

This catches her mother's attention. She turns
on Monroe and glares. "No daughter of mine will
speak to another woman that way."

"Mom, I was just—"

Evelyn silences her with a single look. "No
excuses."

"They're not ladylike," Jameson jumps in.

"I don't care if either of you are ladies. In my
opinion, being a lady in this day and age is highly
overrated, but girls have enough problems without
being catty to one another." She speaks the truth
and we both know it, which is why we all remain
quiet.

"Show Jameson what we picked up today,"
Evelyn suggests after we've all been on our best
behavior for a few minutes.

"He doesn't want to see it, mom." For the first
time since I've known her, there's an embarrassed
edge to Monroe's words. There's no way I'm going
to miss this. I take a step back and watch as she pulls
out some candles and a framed picture.

"I thought it was best if Monroe redid her room
here," Evelyn tells Jameson, her voice tight with
emotion. "I don't want either of you going back to
the penthouse."

I expect them to put up a fight about this but instead they nod. I'd always assumed that Monroe's lack of respect for authority figures stemmed from her father's money. After all, who cares what people think of you when you can just buy their respect, or at least their silence. She's different around her mother. If I hadn't been subjected to such large doses of her bitchiness, I might even like her now.

"I left a few things in the car," Evelyn says to Jameson. "Can you help me with them?"

He glances at me, as if to check that this is okay, but she loops her arm through his.

"Do you mind if I borrow the man of the house?" Sadness coats her words and I can see what a struggle it is for her to keep a smile on her face.

"Of course not." It's not like I can answer any other way.

Plus I've just spent the better part of an hour trying to convince Jameson that I don't need a babysitter. If I want him to believe me and to tell Maddox to step down, then that means I'm going to have to learn to take care of myself in any situation, even those that involve Monroe, a.k.a. The Witched Bitch of the West.

Monroe and I stare at one another. Neither of us speak. She picks up a carrot stick from the tray of crudités her mother has set out for all of us and munches on it. The crunch of her teeth is the only sound in the kitchen, and I join her, absentmindedly eating as a means to pass the time. We might not be capable of being nice to one another, but surely we can shut the hell up and tolerate each other for a few minutes.

"Hugo said you went by the hospital," Monroe says. Apparently, our relationship now includes casual conversation.

"I did," I mumble.

"How did she look? I can't stand to go in there," she admits. "Hospitals aren't my thing."

"You haven't gone to see her?"

Her eyes narrow at the judgment in my tone and I immediately regret my words. "I went," she says defensively. "But only once."

"Yeah. I don't like hospitals, either." I decide to take a different tact. The fact is that Jameson isn't going anywhere. Not if I have anything to say about it. So like it or not, his family is a package deal. Monroe included. As long as I don't have to move into some type of creepy, multi-generational compound with all of them, I need to at least try.

"She looked pale," I say at last. "I didn't stay long. I had no idea Hugo would be there."

"He's always there." Monroe confirms what I had suspected when I saw them. She doesn't have to say any more than that.

"I had no idea they were so close."

"I don't think he did, either," she confesses. "It's funny how you don't realize how you feel about somebody until you don't have a chance to tell them."

Is it opposite day? Because now I find myself wanting to hug her. I refrain, knowing that that would be too much, too soon. It probably always will be.

Jameson and Evelyn reappear, saving us from our uncomfortable attempt at discussion.

"I thought I'd cook dinner this evening." There's a brief glimmer of light in Evelyn West's eyes as she says this, but it immediately extinguishes. She's trying so hard to be strong; anyone can see that. Maybe that's why her kids are treating her with such care.

"Would you like to stay?"

"I'd love to, but I promised my best friend ..."

She waves off my excuse. "No need to explain. Another time."

Jameson's eyes dart to mine and he stops unpacking the grocery bags. "Mom, I'm going to walk Emma to her car."

She nods and begins to discuss what color Monroe would like to paint her bedroom. Jameson doesn't take my hand as he leads me back to my car. "I'm sorry about earlier," he offers.

"But you're still going to have Maddox follow me," I guess.

"You can be mad at me all you want."

"That's good," I jump in, "because I'm going to be."

Reaching out, he cups the side of my face with his palm. "You're a firecracker, Emma Southerly."

I smile sweetly. Just wait until he sees me go off.

Chapter 13

"I'M famous for buying toilet paper now," Josie announces as she slings her purse onto a chair in the corner. "Did you see?"

I glance up from my laptop and grimace. She's holding the bag from Weckman's that The Dealer snapped her with earlier. "I saw."

The real question is whether or not she's thought about what that means. Josie crosses to her dresser and pulls out an oversized t-shirt.

"My boobs are killing me." She strips off her top and bra and pulls the comfy shirt on. "I'm just glad all he caught was the Charmin and not my tampons. Paying Eve's penance is bad enough without photographic evidence."

I close the lid of my computer and search for the right way to bring this up. "So the picture was taken this afternoon?"

"There's the proof." She points to the t.p. sticking out of the plastic bag.

"Did you see anyone? Taking your picture, I mean?" I force myself to ask the hard question.

"No." She lies next to me on the bed and stares up at her bedroom ceiling. I scoot down and join her. Dozens of plastic, glow-in-the-dark stars are still stuck overhead. "Remember when we put those up?"

"Your mom was convinced the landlord was going to kick you out," I remember with a laugh. "What were we, ten?"

"Eleven," Josie corrects me with a giggle. "I abided by the no posters on the wall for a whole year."

"And then you went on a rampage, starting with those." I grab her hand and we look up. When we were younger, we'd lie on the floor during sleep-overs, and I would stare at those stars and make wishes. Right now I wish I still believed in their magic. "Josie, if that photo is from today, someone followed you."

Her grip on my hand tightens as I point this out.

"I know," she whispers. "How didn't I notice him?"

"It's a busy city. Whoever it is knows how to stay unseen." I sigh. It was a long shot that she might remember catching someone with a camera, but we need a break. "Why are you so certain it's a guy?"

"What do you mean?" Josie flips on her side and I do the same. We stare at each other, each clutching a pillow.

"You always say *him* or *he*."

"I guess I just assume this perv is a dude," she says.

The whole game does have a creepy, up-skirt camera vibe. But even narrowing it down to a *him*, doesn't get us any closer to discovering The Dealer's identity.

"You know my pic wasn't the most interesting one he posted. Did you see the other one?"

I frown. The other shot had been nonsensical at best. A cup o' joe labeled May. "The cup of coffee? May? Maybe The Dealer is behind on posting since it's June. "

"No!" Josie sits up and tosses the pillow to the top of the bed. "What was under the cup of coffee."

I roll over and grab my phone from her bedside table. Opening Instagram, I scroll to the photo. "I stared at this thing forever."

"And you didn't notice the business card?" she asks dryly. Leaning over, she taps the screen and I immediately spot the black card poking out from beneath the mug.

"I was looking for lipstick or a logo on the cup." I leave out that I also studied the woodgrain of the table, hoping I might recognize the coffee shop where the photo was taken. I'd been so focused on minute details the whole time, I'd missed the most important element.

"What does it say?" she asks.

I raise an eyebrow. "You noticed but you didn't even try to read it?"

"Not all of us spent our afternoon working on our amateur sleuth badge," she teases. "I figured we'd tackle it later."

I pinch the screen and zoom in. It's hard to make out the card's gold foil lettering, especially since the cup cuts some of the info off. "It looks like a-c-h-è, but I know there's more."

"There's part of a phone number, too."

I sit up on the bed and reach for my laptop. "So we know The Dealer is in Vegas."

"He didn't take any pics of you in California," she says with a nod, "and he was obviously here today."

"That's about the only thing I miss about Palm Springs," I mutter as I open Google. Typing in what I can see on the business card, which is nothing more than the letters and a few digits of a phone number, I hold my breath and hit *search*.

"Anything?" Josies asks as the search results load.

Frowning, I scroll down and stop when I hit the third entry. Cachè. Half the phone number listed matches what I could read on the card. "That can't be a coincidence."

"What?" She worms her way next to me so that she can see the screen. "I don't get it."

"I forgot you failed French."

She jabs me in the stomach. "I didn't take French."

"Cachè means hidden." I give her a second to process this. "Like—"

"The Dealer," she finishes for me. "Holy shit."

"Did I earn my badge?" I ask her.

"With honors."

We both fidget as Cachè's homepage loads. The website is sleek and modern, carefully presented with very little information. "Let's see. They're located in Las Vegas. Big surprise. No clue what they're selling...or hiding."

"Click on that," Josie says, pointing to the company policy page.

The company policy consists of a single line:

Cachè provides singular companionship with uncompromising discretion.

"Wait," Josie fumbles for words as it hits both of us. "Cachè is a brothel."

"I think they use the term escort agency."

"Is there really a difference?"

We both know there is. You don't grow up in Nevada without knowing a bit more about issues of vice than most people your age. "Hand me my phone."

Josie sucks in a breath before she relinquishes it. "Are you sure this is a good idea?"

"You're right. This is why he posted this photo." I check the number on my computer screen as I begin to dial.

"So maybe it's a trap," she says nervously.

"I don't think The Dealer wants to hurt us." I hesitate before I hit the call button. Talking to the agency isn't dangerous. It's just about information, so why is my heart lodged in my throat?

"How do you know that?"

"Because whoever it is followed you around long enough today to get a photo of the most embarrassing part of your day." I tilt my head toward the Weckman's bag.

"Everybody poops, Emma." She jumps on the bed and begins to pace nervously. "What are you going to say?"

"I'm going to wing it," I admit before I press the green circle. It only rings twice before a breathy voice answers.

"Cachè."

"Yes, I'm calling to…" I look at Josie and say the first thing that comes to mind, "Find out about a job."

"YOU'VE OFFICIALLY LOST YOUR MIND," Josie informs me the next morning as we stand in the entry and go over today's plan. "Who is going to notice something like this?"

"Jameson West needs to be taught a lesson." I finish throwing my license in her purse, then pass her mine. I'd borrowed a black, lace romper from her that left little to the imagination. Between the fuck me pumps she'd insisted I wear for today's undercover operation, and handing off my purse, I feel more than a bit out of my element. "Little details are going to be important. Believe me, this Maddox is ex-military."

"What branch?"

"Why do you care, GI Jane?"

She grabs her bag from me and fishes out her plum lipgloss.

"Don't wear that!" I grab it back. "I'd never wear that color."

"You're also not black, Emma," she points out dryly.

"I'm tan and wearing a hat," I shoot back.

She plants her hands on her hips and stares at me. "Hat and tan aside. No one has ever mistaken us for each other."

"As long as you stay far enough from him, he'll never know." I hand her my keys. "Plus, you get to drive the Mercedes."

Offering her the keys to my shiny, new ride was the only part of my insane plan that had interested her.

"You shouldn't go alone."

"It's my only choice unless I want to take Maddox along," I remind her.

"Why do you care if Jameson knows you're playing detective?" she asks, dropping the key chain into my bag.

"I don't. This is about teaching him a lesson."

"Isn't love grand?" she quips, but she doesn't press me further. Neither of us are the type to appreciate a guy overstepping his boundaries. "Just promise me you'll be careful."

"I'm not doing anything dangerous." *Not really*. I've only told her about half of my plans for the day. If Maddox catches up with her, the less she knows, the better.

"Look, he's worried about you, and he has a right to be. I don't see why having a little hired muscle with you is so wrong." She squares her shoulders before she adds, "But I'm your best friend, so lecture over."

I kiss her cheek. "It's cute when you worry. I'll go out the garage. Wait a few minutes and then run out to my car."

With any luck, my newly hired shadow would be too distracted by both of us leaving to realize we'd switched cars.

Climbing into the driver's seat of the Civic, memories flood me. I'd learned to drive in this car courtesy of Josie and Becca. Dad was usually too drunk to give proper instruction. While I'm still not a fan of being behind the wheel, at least I'm comfortable here. I know what every button does. The stereo has a radio and a tape deck. I've never once needed to check a 300 page instruction manual to figure out how to open the fuel tank.

I don't bother to look at Maddox's car as I pull out, but when I finally give in and peek in the rearview mirror, I see he's starting to pull away from the curb. Dammit, he must assume we're together. He's a few car lengths behind me when he comes to a stop. Josie's in the Mercedes, heading the opposite direction at breakneck speed.

"I hope I have full insurance on that," I say to myself. But her dramatic exit works. Maddox backs his car into a driveway and peels out to catch up with her. I blow a kiss.

It might be nice to think the hard part of the day is behind me, but I left a few errands off the list I shared with Josie when I convinced her to help me with my shenanigans.

Pulling over a few blocks away, I glance around to make certain that Maddox didn't wise up. When I know I'm alone, I dig Dominic Chamber's card from my wallet and input his address in my phone's GPS app. He's only fifteen minutes away, which gives me plenty of time to pay him a visit and still make my interview at Cachè.

With a full day of being in the wrong place at

the right time ahead of me, I can't help hoping that I'll catch the attention of The Dealer. I failed to mention to Josie that today I'll be playing the role of live bait. If this amateur creep is interested in photos of Josie with toilet paper, I can only imagine how eager he'll be to catch me walking into an escort agency. This time, though, I'll be the one waiting to snap a picture of him.

Reaching into Josie's purse, I rifle through a handful of receipts from Weckman's until I find a few lipsticks stashed at the bottom. Pulling the caps off each, I search for the perfect color. The last one labeled Troublemaker is exactly what I'm searching for. Swiping the bright red over my lips, I smack them together in the mirror. The Dealer has no idea who he's messed with.

"Say cheese, asshole."

Chapter 14

THE CHAMBER DETECTIVE Agency looks like the set for an old film noir. Right down to the gold foil letters on the office door. A bell tinkles as I open it and look around to discover a cluttered desk and a half-dead fern. A familiar head pokes around the corner.

"Just a sec. You want coffee?" he calls out.

"No thanks." I don't trust my stomach to keep anything, even something as innocuous as coffee, down today. Butterflies are already churning up what's left of last night's late night snack with Josie.

I remember Dominic Chamber more for his woolly eyebrows than his detection skills. It's a long shot coming to him for help, especially given that he hadn't been keen enough to spot a fake Babe Ruth card. But since I don't know any other private investigators, he's what I have to work with.

Today he's in a velour jogging suit the color of overly cooked green beans. How he manages to wear it and keep the office at a balmy 85 degrees is beyond me. I fan myself with my hand as he pushes aside a stack of papers to make room for his coffee mug.

"Let me guess…cheating boyfriend?" he asks, sizing me up.

"Close," I grant him. "Cheating wife." Amongst so many other things, but I have to start somewhere.

"Well, the times, they're a-changing." He leans back in his chair and crosses his arms behind his nearly bald head. "Do I know you?"

"We had some business before." I hesitate to mention the baseball card. A shrewd business man doesn't accept payment in the form of collectibles.

"Hold on," he says before I can continue. "I'm good with faces." A few seconds later, he snaps his fingers. "The waitress from the Golden Nugget."

If we were playing hot and cold, he'd be in the arctic. I shake my head.

"The lady with the lost Shih Tzu."

Arguably I'm about to lose my Shih Tzu just being here, but I can see that he's not going to stop guessing. "The girl from the pawn shop."

"The heartbreaker." He clutches his chest. Then he points to a frame on the far wall. I look over to find the forged card on display. "I decided who cares if it's real. It impresses clients."

"You know what? I think I need to be some-where." I grab my purse from the floor, but before I can stand up, he starts to talk.

"That's not your purse," he tells me, "or your outfit. I'd wager you're as comfortable in that lipstick as you are in those heels. You're pretending to be someone else today, which means you're hiding from someone. Maybe your mother? She's the cheating wife, right? But you work in your father's shop, so why would you care?"

My mouth falls open and I have to force it closed. "How did you do that?"

"I might be bad with faces, but I'm good with details."

"No, really," I press. I don't think private investi-gators cling to their secrets as tightly as magicians, and I want to know his tricks.

"You looked at the floor for a second before you picked up the purse, like you were looking for a different one. You've been tugging up your top since you walked in. Whoever that belongs to has a smaller bust-line. No offense."

"None taken," I assure him. "Go on."

"I didn't recognize you at first because you don't look like the kid who threw that fake card in my face."

"Sorry," I interject, but he waves me off.

Taking a sip of coffee, he studies me for a moment. "Hiding from your mom is a guess. Girls your age like to dress up behind their mother's backs. I'm guessing she wouldn't want you walking around this city looking like that. No offense again."

At least, I'll look the part at the escort agency.

"You said cheating wife and I remembered that the other guy who works at that shop, who is less concerned about authenticity, by the way, mentioned the owner was out. He'd been coming in less since he got divorced. I gathered since you're here about a cheating wife and your parents are divorced that we're talking about your mom."

"Holy shit." I applaud politely and he bows his head.

"So what can I help you with, Miss?"

"Emma," I correct him. "Can I still call you Dominic?"

He nods, steepling his fingers as he waits for me to spill.

"It's about my sister," I begin. "She's...she died."

"I'm sorry to hear that."

"Anyway, I came across her death certificate recently and noticed that there's no father listed on it." I really hope his gift extends to reading between the lines, so I don't have to spell out anymore of this than I have to.

"And you want to know who her dad is? You thought you shared the same father," he guessed.

"Yes," I say in a quiet voice.

"I have to warn you, Emma. Paternity cases can dredge up some nasty secrets."

I think of how much my father drinks to deal with her death. Then to Hans and his unnerving relationship with Becca. "There are a lot of things I don't know about my sister. I have to start somewhere."

"I'll look into it." He picks up a card from a stack on his desk but I shake my head.

"I already have one."

"Then I'll just need you to fill this out. Basic information. Your name. Her name. Everything is kept confidential." He passes me a sheet of paper and a pen. "My standard rate is $100 an hour."

I flinch and force a smile. "Do you take credit cards?"

"And fake baseball cards," he says, grinning back.

I finish filling out the information form and check the time on my phone. "I have to go!"

"I look forward to working together," he calls after me. "I'll let you know as soon as I have anything."

I pause at the door and consider my next request. "There's one more thing," I say slowly. "My father had a grudge against Nathaniel West. I want to know how it started."

"It might raise some eyebrows if I go digging

around looking for info on Nathaniel West," he warns me.

I think about my next appointment. "Be discreet."

CACHÈ IS NOT what I expect. The agency's office is as minimal as their website, the only sign of personality is the black paint coating the walls. But I guess you hide things in the dark. There's only one woman inside and she greets me at the door. Her dress suit matches the wall, the neckline dipping to display an impressive amount of cleavage. Other than a single silver streak at each temple her hair is fiery red.

"You must be Caroline." She extends a hand and I take it uncertainly. "I'm Suzanne."

"Um, yes, I am." I'd nearly forgotten the fake name I'd fed her when I made the appointment.

"If you don't mind my asking…" She pauses and I suspect whatever comes out of her mouth next is going to be a bit rude. "…how old are you?"

"I'll be eighteen next week." That isn't a lie. "Is that a problem?"

It's been a while since I brushed up on the Vegas prostitution guidelines. It's a joke at Belle Mère Prep that they hand out a pamphlet on the subject during career day in the local public schools.

"Oh, lovely!" She claps her hands together in delight, which I suppose means I'm good to *ho*. "You won't be able to start until then, of course, but we can begin all the necessary paperwork and tests."

"Tests?" I repeat back.

"The usual. We need to check for STDs and pregnancy as well as overall health." She gestures to the chair at her desk. I sit down and let this soak in. I don't know how far I'll have to go to find out why The Dealer led us here. Getting blood drawn might be my hard limit, never mind having someone poke around inside my vagina. Ironically. "Will that be a problem?"

"I guess I didn't realize that…" My blush finishes the sentence for me.

"Sexual relations are not a requirement. This is an escort agency." She gives me a practiced smile that feels as rehearsed as those lines. "You choose if you want to engage in sex with your clients."

"Then why the tests?"

Her smile grows forced. "Many of our girls enjoy sexual relations with our clients who are very wealthy men and *very appreciative*."

Translation: they're willing to pay because they're old, fat, or desperate.

"As I mentioned, we don't encourage our girls to have sex, but…"

"I don't have a problem with it," I interject

before she can end the interview. It's not like I'm actually taking the job, so what do I care about the semantics of it. "I just wanted to understand. I don't want to get into trouble."

"There will be no trouble." The warmth in her tone returns as she begins to click around with her mouse. "Our clients are very discreet. They know to expect a certain caliber of women and they follow the rules."

"If they don't?"

"I handle all appointments personally. Once you're on my blacklist, you can't beg or buy yourself off it."

I don't want to know what lands you on that list, judging by the cold undercurrent in her words.

"You'll want to choose a name," she advises. "We don't recommend that girls give their real names. It encourages stalking or romance, both activities we strictly prohibit."

So I'm not allowed to fall in love with the desperate old men. I think I can handle that. "So I can work here?"

I'm surprised by how little she needs to know to hire me. Then again, I think living, breathing, with a vagina might be the only non-negotiables.

"We'll have to wait for the tests and your birthday, but I think you're just what a few of my clients are looking for." She pushes her chair away from the desk. "Excuse me, while I get some forms off the printer."

She walks into the other room and I'm left with a choice. Since I don't have any time to waste, I gamble. Jumping up, I lean over her desk and grab her mouse. I click around until I find the appointments calendar on her desktop. Opening it, I scroll until I find what I'm looking for.

May.

Whoever she is, she's popular, because she's booked out through the end of the next week. Before I can talk myself out of it, I schedule a fake name in the next available time slot. I use my real number. Hopefully, they don't call to confirm bookings like the hair salon. The only thing left to decide is where, and I happen to have an in at the West Resort. It's going to be fun to explain this one to Jameson. I'm clicking finish when the screen freezes. Shooting daggers at the wheel of death that's replaced the mouse's curser, I count the seconds until it stops and I can close the schedule. I've just sat back down when Suzanne reappears.

"This has all your forms as well as the clinic information. Call and tell them Suzanne sent you when you make your appointment."

I nod as she continues, but my mind is elsewhere.

"Do you have any questions, Caroline? *Caroline*?"

It takes me a hot minute to remember she's

talking to me. "Sorry. I started thinking about having my blood drawn," I lie. "I hate it."

"A necessary precaution." She passes the folder to me as she shows me to the door, then she winks. "I think you'll find it's worth it."

Chapter 15

MADDOX IS WAITING for me in the driveway, and it doesn't take me long to figure out how he knows we switched. Josie leans against the side of his car, wrapping a lock of hair around her finger and giggling. The girl could give lessons on how to flirt. I can't help but admire the scene. If my bodyguard is upset about the bait and switch, she's thoroughly distracted him. Then again, when I press the garage door button, he whips around and glares at me.

Busted.

I pull the car inside and brace myself as I get out. I knew there'd be a price to pay for my little stunt.

"Do you understand that when you pull shit like that I get in trouble?" Maddox yells at me as soon as I'm out of the garage. Veins pulse in his meaty neck as he continues, "I like my job. I like to eat."

For a second I imagine what it takes to feed him in a day: a couple dozen eggs, maybe a few whole chickens. He's that big. In past centuries, his ancestors were probably mistaken for gods. I swallow hard before I respond. "I'm sorry, but I tried to tell Jameson that I didn't want to be followed."

"So instead you made me look like a fool." Maddox crosses his arms and glares at me. "I'm going to have to tell him what happened."

That I expected. Part of me is surprised that he hasn't already been in contact with Jameson. "When you talk to him remind him that I'm his girlfriend not his child."

"I don't care if you're his prize canary, he hired me to protect you," Maddox grumbles.

"You don't have to tell him," Josie suggests. She moves to Maddox's side and strokes his shoulder. She practically has to stand on her tiptoes to reach it. I shoot her a warning look that she ignores with a shrug. "If he doesn't know, you can't get in trouble."

"That's very sweet of you, Miss Deckard." Maddox softens in her presence, shifting from a hardened military man to a cuddly teddy bear. It's simply further proof of Josie's magic touch in the man department. He smiles down at her but then he puffs out his chest as if to remind both of them what a big badass he is. "I have a duty, though."

"To protect and serve the highest bidder," I

mutter under my breath. Thankfully, he's too mesmerized by my best friend to notice.

"I'm going in," I announce loudly in the hopes that I can convince Josie to stop playing with her new toy and come with me. There's so much to tell her.

"You have my phone number," Josie reminds him. She scampers into the house behind me, laughing. "You didn't tell me he was such a pushover."

"I'm not certain his training included warding off horny, teenage girls," I say dryly.

Josie wags her finger at me, but her lips twitch with a grin. "Hey, I resemble that remark."

We're still teasing each other when we walk in on Josie's mom in the living room. Well, not just her mom, but rather her mom kissing some guy. Josie halts on the spot and gasps. I do my best to shush her but the couple pulls apart.

"Oh girls, I didn't expect you home so soon!" She swipes at her smeared lipstick, doing her best to straighten her bunched skirt.

"School's out for the summer," Josie informs her. "You're lucky I was out."

"I saw Emma's notes," she says, obviously flustered.

I shoot Josie an apologetic look. After showing up at the ass-crack of dawn the other day, I thought it would be more courteous to give Marion a heads up on when I would and wouldn't be here.

"Hi." I step in to try to smooth over the situation. "I'm Emma."

Marion's date takes my outstretched hand tentatively. I can't decide if he's shy or if he's never seen a girl shake hands before. Either way, his palms are sweaty and when no one's looking I wipe my own hand on my romper.

"Emma, this is Anton." Marion smiles affectionately as she introduces the new man in her life. Anton for his part is as nondescript as they come except for two defining characteristics: thinning brown hair and round glasses that lean more toward spectacles than most modern eye wear.

When no one speaks again and Josie doesn't step forward to introduce herself, I take the initiative. "What do you do?"

"I'm an accountant." He sighs as he tells me. "Not very exciting, I guess."

Considering that my life could use a whole lot less excitement at the moment, I think dating an accountant sounds pretty sexy.

"Can I make you guys a snack?" Marion offers, tapping her finger nails together like a broken clock.

"We already ate," Josie says coldly.

I don't bother to correct her, even though I could go for a bite. If she isn't careful, we'll be making a pilgrimage to In-N-Out later to rectify the situation. Josie stomps down the hall and slams her bedroom door shut behind her.

When I duck into her room, Josie shuts the door softly behind me, then leans against it.

"What's wrong?" I ask.

"That guy," she whispers, and I lean in so that she can keep her conspiracy on the DL. "I dated him a few weeks ago."

I suck in a breath and try to think of something reassuring to say. It's pretty hard given that I want to yell at her. I have been waiting for this to happen; a single mom, who even I have to admit is a MILF, and her teenage daughter with a taste for older men, adds up to either a really bad sitcom or a really good V.C. Andrews novel.

"Let me have it," she says when I stay quiet.

"Sheesh, Josie! You have to have seen this coming. I don't know where to begin!"

"Maybe with the fact that this is all my fault," Josie suggests. "That you knew this was going to happen and it was only a matter of time until trouble?"

"Sounds like you have it covered. Let me know when you need me to jump in."

Her lower lip begins to tremble and I immediately regret what I just said. "What am I going to do?"

"Look, he can't have known, and now that he's seen you he's going to break up with her."

"Mom really likes him and I fucked it up."

"Um, he really likes seventeen-year-old girls. I'm

not entirely certain that you're not doing her a favor."

"He didn't know how old I was. I lied about my age," she admits.

"Do you do that with all of them?"

"The nice ones," she says. "Some of them like knowing that I'm younger."

I shudder, thinking about that. I pat the bed next to me and she comes over to sit down. "So, he was a nice one?"

"Yeah." It's not like her to be so quiet, but, then again, she's not usually sorry about who she dates.

"Then he's going to break up with her, and if he doesn't, then we'll figure it out," I promise.

She rests her head on my shoulder, her curly locks tickling my neck.

"Besides, I have lots of things to tell you that I promise will prove a distraction."

"Oh," she claps her hands and jumps to her feet. Scientists should study how rapidly her moods swing. "I want to hear all about it but first I'm going to go to the bathroom, okay?"

I nod. Now that Maddox has figured out our little ploy, there's no need to keep up our Parent Trap pretense. By now, he'll have delivered news of my shenanigans to Jameson, who'll hopefully take the hint that I'm not putting up with a bodyguard.

I grab my purse and start taking out Josie's stuff from our earlier switcheroo. Before I can throw her phone on the bed, a notification pops up for Instagram. It takes me a second to remember what her lock screen code is, but before I can see what photographic delights our friendly, anonymous stalker has in store for us, Josie reappears and snatches it from my hands.

"What the hell are you doing?"

"Um, looking at your phone." It seems obvious to me, but given the shock registered on her face I guess maybe it's not to her.

"I didn't tell you you could look at my phone."

"What crawled up your snatch?" I ask her.

"You!" she shrieks. "First you sit there and judge me after I've given you a place to sleep, even though you're keeping things from me."

Okay, she's totally lost it. Hadn't she been fine minutes ago? "I'm not keeping anything from you!"

"Oh, like where were you going today that I couldn't tag along?"

"Somewhere where I needed my bodyguard not to go," I remind her. "I was about to tell you everything I did."

"Save it, Emma. Ever since you met Jameson West you've been a different person."

Standing up, I dump the contents of her purse on the bed and grab my phone and wallet. She's being totally unreasonable. "You think I'm judging you?"

"I know you're judging me, but you're too nice to even say it to my face."

"Fine!" I explode. "You treat these little romances of yours like games and you always knew someone was going to get hurt. This time it's your mom. What happens when you ruin someone's marriage or get some poor schmuck arrested?"

"I'm going to be eighteen soon." She dismisses my argument with a roll of her eyes.

"But you weren't always eighteen. How old do these guys even think you are? Wait, don't answer that because I really don't want to know anything more about this."

"Of course you don't because you just want to pretend you're my best friend."

I have absolutely no clue how things escalated this quickly. A few minutes ago she was leaning on me for support and I was preparing to spill my guts about everything that happened in Palm Springs. Now I'm glad I hadn't. This betrayal cuts deeper than the others I experienced this summer, which is saying something. She's being irrational, but I'm not going to waste my time telling her that. "I thought I could count on you."

"You can. Here's a little judgement for you," she offers when I reach her bedroom door. "You have a boyfriend accused of murder who's hired a body-guard to stalk you. Your step daddy is a movie producer and you're driving a brand new Mercedes. Stop acting like we should all feel sorry for you."

"Because my life is so perfect," I hiss. "You have no idea how hard things have been."

"Save it, Emma. If I want a dose of reality I'll take a look at my own life."

"Then I suggest you do that soon," I throw open the door. I rush out of the house past a startled Marion and her new boyfriend slash Josie's ex. As soon as I'm out the front door, I run directly into Jameson's chest, but I don't feel like being comforted by him right now.

"Get off me," I shove him and hurry down the sidewalk.

"Where are you going?" he demands.

"None of your goddamn business," I call over my shoulder.

"Emma, wait!"

But I don't listen. I jump in the car and back out, nearly running him over in the process. From now on no one is going to stop me, no one is going to make choices for me, and no one is going to tell me what to do.

Chapter 16

THE NICE THING about Las Vegas is that if you drive fast enough for long enough, you'll hit the desert. Then you can drive as angrily as you need to.

I don't bother to look at my odometer when I reach open road, all I know is that the Mercedes has sports mode and I'm going to put it through all its paces. I don't have to check behind me to know that Jameson is following. Maybe he gave Maddox the day off and decided he'd do the job himself. But either my car isn't as fast as his BMW or he just knows how to work his better because after a few minutes he pulls alongside me driving the wrong direction. He casts a furious glance my way and then cuts ahead of me.

I resist the urge to speed up when his brake lights flicker on. He's slowing us down, no doubt forcing me to come to a stop, but I'm not going to make this easy on him. Too many things have been handed to Jameson in his life. If he wants me he's going to have to fight for me.

Glancing down, I discover that he's slowed us down to about thirty miles per hour. I've just decided to stop fighting him, when he races forward and screeches to a halt allowing the back of his car to slide so that he's blocking the road entirely. I slam on my own brakes and jump out of the car.

"What the hell do you think you're doing? Do you know how dangerous that is?"

"Please give me a lecture," he retorts, "when you're racing through Las Vegas going a hundred miles per hour!"

At another time that might have embarrassed me. I don't want to explain to him how I'm feeling. That I needed to get away from Josie's house and Belle Mère and this whole mess as quickly as possible. Two days with the car and I've already started treating it like a toy.

"We all have to die sometime," I say with a shrug.

"You don't mean that." I open my mouth to protest this, but he keeps going. "And if you do, then we have bigger problems. What you did was reckless."

"I know." I cross my arms over my chest, unable to ignore the wave of guilt that overcomes me.

Speed had been a factor in Becca's death. It's one of the reasons I didn't want to drive. I didn't want the power of a car in my hands. The second I'd gotten one, I abused it. "I'll get rid of the car."

"I'm not talking about the car, Duchess." His gaze drops to the ground and he shakes his head, his frustration with me only making me feel worse. "I'm talking about tricking Maddox."

"That was for your own good," I informed him.

"Exactly how is putting yourself in danger for my own good?" His blue eyes flash like the tip of a flame and he lunges forward grabbing me by the arm. "Do you have any idea how much danger you're in?"

"Do you?" I ask him.

"I guess I do since I'm smart enough to realize that if someone pushed you through a window, then you know something."

"I don't!" I scream. "This whole thing is a giant mix-up and I'm tired of trying to keep everything straight. We're all tangled together like a big bowl of noodles. I can't tell which lies are mine and which belong to other people anymore."

"Slow down and start from the beginning. Is there anything you haven't told me?"

I glower at him, but he may as well know. "I overheard something at your house that night. When I confronted Leighton about it—"

"Wait, what did you overhear?"

I wave off his question. "It's not important."

"Like hell it isn't!" he growls.

"Get your caveman in check," I warn him, "or I'm not telling you anything."

Jameson steps back and runs both his hands through his copper waves. He pauses like that, as if he's considering pulling out his own hair, but he waits for me to continue.

"I overheard something. I asked Leighton about it, someone pushed us."

"But you aren't in danger," he mutters. "What did she tell you?"

"Nothing. She never got a chance to."

He looks to the sky as if pleading with the Gods for patience. Then he turns the full force of his smoldering gaze on me. I can't say no to that look, not when it's coupled with his strong jawline and insane good looks.

"What did you want to find out from her?" He rephrases the question.

If I tell him what I overheard, he'll know I doubted him. I make a choice knowing that I can't quite anticipate what the consequences will be. "She was talking to Monroe, something about that she had seen what had happened and she was protecting *him*."

"Who is *him*?" Jameson asks in confusion.

"To be honest, I assumed it was you, at first."

"Go on," he says after a moment of silence that

seems to extend farther than the desert surrounding us.

"I thought she was talking about you. She was telling Monroe that she had seen what had happened, but that she wasn't going to tell anyone what he had done."

"And you thought she was talking about me killing my father?"

"I didn't know what to think. Everything was chaos. You'd just been arrested and—"

"You don't have to explain yourself," he stops me in a soft voice, but the disappointment in his tone says otherwise.

"I only wanted to know what she was talking about. When I confronted her, she told me they'd been talking about Jonas."

"You told me that night you believed I was innocent, but you still jumped to that conclusion." He's not interested in what Leighton might know about Jonas, only in what conclusions I'd drawn about him.

"I did. I still do," I whisper.

"Why?" It's less of a question and more of a plea. "I don't understand how you can believe me. Sometimes I don't even believe myself."

"Don't say that." I move toward him but he looks away.

"I'm no good for you."

The sincerity in his words makes my heart sink.

I grab his chin and force him to face me. "You're the best thing that's ever happened to me."

"How can you say that? Your dad hates me. I spend most of my time worrying so much about your safety that I hired someone to follow you, and you've been dragged into a murder investigation. I've done nothing to deserve you."

"You set me free," I whisper. "I didn't have a life before you. I refused to have one. I'd just accepted that nothing was ever going to change and had half-buried myself in other people's trinkets at the store. Then you changed everything."

"Out here"—he glances around before returning his gaze to mine—"I can see for miles in any direction, but right now, all I see is you. I think you're the only thing I've ever seen clearly."

I don't need him to explain, because it's exactly how I feel.

He takes a single step forward, closing the short space between us. "I love you, Emma Southerly."

It takes a moment for his words to soak into me. I've known I loved him for a while now, but hearing him say it, I can't find the words to respond.

Jameson doesn't wait for me to respond, he continues, "I think I fell in love with you when you walked into my kitchen and made me that macaroni and cheese."

"And you've made me work for it all this time?"

I tease, sniffing as the first tears break loose and stream down my cheeks.

He brushes them away. "I can't be held accountable for acting crazy; you've driven me to it."

"Okay," I croak. For now, I'll concede on that point. It's not as if I've been the picture of mental health since we met. I guess that's why they say crazy in love. "I love you, too."

He heaves a sigh. "I don't know if I deserve that."

"Shut up and accept it," I order him. Grabbing a fistful of his t-shirt, I pop onto my toes and offer him my lips. His face slants over mine and he captures them like he's captured my heart.

We stumble toward the car. Jameson feels around behind me, refusing to break off the kiss until he finds the door handle. He lays me across the back seat of the Mercedes before he creeps over me. My hand snakes around his neck, drawing our lips together again, as our bodies mold to one another.

Reaching down, I fumble as I try to unfasten his jeans. He groans and the sound of it vibrates through me. "Not in the car, Duchess."

"Jameson," I pull back and address him seriously, "I don't think I can wait any longer."

He laughs at my earnestness. "Which one of us is the guy again?"

"Let's take off our pants and find out." I wiggle

my hips, hoping that he won't be able to resist my suggestion.

"I swear to god that the minute you turn eighteen, I'm going to find the nearest bed and take my sweet time claiming you."

"Claiming me?" I repeat.

He rocks his hips against me, sending a thrill pulsating between my legs. "Do you have a problem with that?"

"Claiming sounds good," I murmur, "but I don't want to wait."

"It will be worth it," he promises me.

Of that, I have no doubt. It's more of a patience thing. The trouble is that I don't have any left.

"I need you, Jamie." The nickname appears on my tongue and it's like it's been there my whole life —like he's been here my whole life.

"We don't have to wait for everything," he reassures me, pushing a renegade strand of hair from my face.

I arch my body against his, wondering if he can really hold out. His arm circles my waist and he holds me like that. Blood rushes to my head as he leans forward and catches the top of my strapless romper in his teeth. I'm beginning to see spots in my vision when he tugs it down, freeing my breasts. I strain to change position, so I can see what's happening, but when the heat of his mouth closes over my nipple, I go limp. He sucks it past his teeth, swirling the tip of his tongue around the swiftly hardening peak.

"I've waited my whole life for you, Duchess," he tells me as he releases it. "When this is over, I'm going to take you away from here."

"Where?" I murmur dreamily, ready to imagine what our life together will be like then.

"It doesn't matter," he teases, "because you won't see anything other than the bed."

I moan loudly as he follows that promise by taking my other nipple in his mouth. He lingers there, not trying to stop me as I begin to buck my hips against his to seek relief.

"That's it," he coaxes and I feel his free hand press between my legs. He pushes aside the scrap of lace that passes for shorts and runs his fingers down me. I feel one gently push inside and a throaty cry escapes me as he moves it in and out. "God, you are so tight. I'm going to have to do this as often as possible before your birthday."

"Promise?" I breathe. It's the only word that I can force out as he continues.

"Of course, Duchess. Now let go."

I feel another finger stretching me and that's all it takes. Jameson holds me as I release, his forehead pressed in the valley between my breasts as I ride out the gift he's just given me.

When I've regained control of my body, I smile shyly at him. "Your turn."

This time he doesn't argue. Instead, he licks his lips and unbuttons his pants. I scramble onto my knees but before I can return the favor the chime of an incoming text message interrupts.

"Ignore it," I command him just as his phone chimes again. When the third message chimes before I have his pants down, I sit back and wait for him to check his texts.

"Levi and his goddam timing," Jameson grumbles when he sees his phone. "Apparently, I have a house guest."

Now seems like a good time to mention that he's going to have another one. It's probably also the right time to tell him that he needs to kick Levi Rowe to the curb. Even through my oxygen-drenched brain, I know I have to do something before Levi finds out something he shouldn't.

Jameson pockets his phone and lounges back. "He can wait."

"I don't think that's a good idea," I say hurriedly. "Plus, there are beds at your house."

He raises an eyebrow. "I thought I was clear about that."

He was crystal clear about it. I'm beginning to think his checklist is even more rigid than mine. "I was thinking we could practice. Clothes on or maybe clothes off and *everything but*."

"It's going to be really hard to drive across town with blue balls."

I bite my lip and pout, remembering what he told me the other day. "Why are we in two separate cars?"

"Because someone wanted to race," he reminds me.

"We can leave mine here," I suggest, tracing the bulging outline in his pants, "and come back for it later."

"Seems like a lot of trouble." His breathing speeds up as I shake my head.

"I promise it will be worth it."

He doesn't argue with me any further. Jameson pulls my car off the road. "If anything happens to it, I'll buy you a new one."

I'm not in the least bit worried about what happens to that car, even though I have to admit that I like having my own set of wheels. I get into the passenger seat of the BMW.

"Buckle up," he demands as he shifts the car into drive and heads toward the city.

"I can't," I inform him. "Drive carefully. Oh, and Jameson, see if you can hold out."

Then I wiggle under the arm controlling the gear shift and give him no choice but to lose that challenge.

Chapter 17

THIS TIME when we arrive at Jameson's Belle Mère estate, I take a longer look. This home is modeled after a Mediterranean villa complete with tiled roof and a large fountain out front. I'd noticed that the last time I was here, but I hadn't been able to appreciate the details like I do now. If he told me that it had been dug up from an ancient village in Tuscany, I would believe it.

I let out a low whistle. "Impressive. So let's see, you have the penthouse at the top of the casino, a chalet up on Mt. Charleston, and a villa in town. Any other properties you want to tell me about?"

"There's the flat in London," he teases me. "Amongst others."

"Do you have a book I can peruse or..."

"I'd rather surprise you by taking you to each one."

I have to admit that I like the sound of that. He parks his BMW in the drive. I've learned to stay put until he opens my door. Everyone's always bitching that chivalry is dead. If he's its last dying breath, I'm not going to be the one to extinguish it. He takes my hand as soon as I'm out and we head inside the house.

We've just stepped into the foyer when my phone rings. "That's my mom," I tell him, recognizing the ring tone. "I can only avoid her for so long before she sicks the police department on me. I've spent enough quality time with the Belle Mère PD to last me a couple of years."

"Take the call, I'll find Levi." He gives me a swift kiss before he heads off in the direction of the kitchen. One simple gesture and he's left me breathless. I'm in so much trouble with him.

"Hi mom," I greet her.

"Where are you?"

"Nice to talk to you, too." I turn toward an empty room that serves as some type of parlor, hoping no one else will hear my conversation with her. "I'm in Belle Mère."

"I've been trying to reach your father but—"

"I'm not staying with him," I stop her. There's no point in trying to keep the facts from her. I hear a sharp inhale on the other line.

"Where are you staying?"

"With Josie." It's not exactly a lie. I haven't

brought up my fight with her to Jameson yet, so I don't know for sure that he'll let me stay here. If he doesn't, I guess I'll be begging her forgiveness after dark.

"Emma," she says in a warning tone.

"Call Marion if you don't believe me," I snap.

"Fine. Did you get your car at least?" Trust my mother to segue into a topic that makes her look good. She's doing damage control without knowing what caused the destruction in the first place.

"I did. It's nice."

"Maybe you could drive back down here and pick up your stuff," she suggests.

"Mom," I say it slowly, wanting to catch her attention. "I won't be coming back to Palm Springs unless Hans is out of town." I add the qualifier because as angry as I am with her, I know it's not her fault.

"Emma, what happened between you and Hans?" she asks in a soft voice.

And here it is. My chance to tell her the truth. But before I can, I remember Josie's face this afternoon after she saw Anton with her mother. She'd stepped over a line and she couldn't turn back. If I tell my mother, I know she'll side with me. I also know there's a prenup, that there will be a nasty divorce and that she'll have her heart broken all over again. She has to suspect what kind of man she's married to. She can't possibly know the depths of his depravity, though, and I'm not ready to be the one to tell her. Not yet. "I saw the script for Hans's movie." It's as good of a reason as any. "There's a sex scene in there between me and Jameson."

There's a long pause on the other end of the line.

"Did you have sex with him that night?" she asks.

I had no idea she was capable of such directness. "No, I didn't. I told Hans that, but he refuses to take it out."

"Honey, you can't make business decisions—"

Here come the apologetics. I've given her enough slack for the evening. "Mom, sorry, I need to go. Something's come up."

I hang up before she can stop me and turn the ringer off on my phone. Tonight I only want to be with Jameson. But as I round the corridor that leads to the kitchen, I realize that might be harder than I thought.

The gang's all here.

"I guess I shouldn't be surprised that I didn't get an invitation," I say to Monroe. She doesn't even bother to answer me. I suppose the brief moment we had the other day was a fluke.

Unlike the others, Jonas has the decency to come over to me.

"Good to see you," he says, hugging me awkwardly. It's hard to admit there was a time when

I would have bottled up that momentary contact and clung to it for months. Finally being over Jonas, I'm having a hard time not judging how pitifully I'd acted.

I break away as soon as it's polite. "I saw you at the hospital."

"I'm sorry?"

"A few days ago." I attempt to jog his memory, but he still stares at me blankly. Then again, he's always been a bit of a beautiful nothing. Seeing him now, I can't help but wonder what Leighton felt the need to protect him from. "Did you go to visit Leighton?"

"No." He grabs a beer out of a six pack on the counter. "I just got back in town."

"You know what? Hugo mentioned that." He's not going to budge, so either he forgot or he's protecting himself as well. What does Jonas have to hide? "I guess I thought it was you."

I'm absolutely positive that I'd spotted Jonas at Belle Pointe, but why is he covering it up? Sure, his story is that he was out of town, but I know better. I might not always be great with names or facts, but faces I'm pretty good at—especially one I've nearly sucked the lips off.

"Trying to steal my girl?" Levi swaggers over and drops an arm around my shoulder with the confidence of a man who knows what's going to greet him when he looks in the mirror. Any other time, I might be flattered by his attention, but I saw that headshot in my stepfather's office, and I suspect Levi isn't at Casa de West to catch up with the family.

I shrug away from him and force a small smile. "Good to see you."

Judging from the scathing glare that Sabine, Monroe's less nice best friend gives me, he won't have a hard time finding another girl to feed his ego. She saunters over and wedges herself in the space between us. If she knew I was grateful that she's acting as a buffer, she'd probably lock me in a room with him. Sabine's bizarre need to look out for her own interests is only trumped by her uncompromising policy that the rest of humanity remain below her.

I take my chances anyway, knowing how much it will irk her, and lean to whisper in her ear. "Thanks. I couldn't get away from him to find my boyfriend."

The only thing that might annoy Sabine more than knowing that she's helped me is a reminder that I've landed Jameson West. Now that I've put that pot on to boil, I hurry away.

Jameson is nowhere to be seen, which sucks considering I'm stuck in the high school reunion from hell: ex-boyfriend, guy I slept with to get back at ex-boyfriend, ex-boyfriend's girlfriend, the first female anti-christ, and the hot guy planning to screw over one of his best friends for fame. I guess Friday nights are alright for fighting.

I duck out onto the back patio. Leave it to the Wests to eschew the traditional barbecue grill and picnic table and replace it with a full grotto, a gourmet outdoor kitchen, and not one, not two, but *three* guest houses on the far side of the pool's stone waterfall.

"Subtle," I mutter to myself.

A door opens behind me, but when I glance over my shoulder, my heart sinks. It isn't Jameson.

"Care to go for a swim?" Levi flashes me his signature smile.

"I don't have a suit."

He leans against a stone column and chuckles. "I've never found that to be a problem."

"I'm guessing you don't find many things to be a problem," I say to him. *Like your conscience, for instance.*

He blinks, looking a bit confused, then shrugs. "Do you mind if I swim?"

"Go right ahead, but I'm not jumping in if you start to drown."

Levi clutches his chest. "You wound me. What did I do to offend you so terribly, Emma...?" He pauses, trying to remember my last name.

"Southerly," I offer it to him, for reasons I can't even fathom. It's that goddamn charismatic grin of his.

He strips his t-shirt over his head, but before he

can take off his pants, I think better of the situation. "Actually, I do care if you swim."

His fingers freeze on the button of his shorts. "I didn't take you for being a shy one."

"I'm not," I reassure him. "But I do have a shred of decency."

"I can keep my shorts on," he says, but I shake my head.

"That's not what this is about, Levi. When are you going to tell Jameson the truth?"

"I don't know what you mean." So that's how he's going to play it.

"You're going to have to lie better than that if you're going to land an award for playing him in 'Wild West.'" I make sure to put the title in air quotes.

"How do you know about that?" he demands.

"I'm guessing Jameson didn't fill you in on who my stepfather is."

When he continues his impression of total vacancy, I sigh and continue. "Hans Von Essen. Ring a bell?"

"Holy shit. I had no clue."

"Yeah." I put a hand up to stop him. "I guessed that from the fact you were stupid enough to come here."

"Why would it be stupid to visit an old friend?" There's definitely no Academy Award in his future. Maybe he finds it easier to act on screen than he does to lie to someone's face. Either way, he's charismatic, but he's not convincing.

"I find being lied to pretty insulting," I inform him.

"I'm not lying to you. I just came to catch up, and study his mannerisms, and find out how his family is doing," he continues and I see now that he's lying to himself. I suppose you'd have to, to betray a friend so deeply. "So what if I want to get him just right? Whoever plays Jameson should be emotionally true."

"Save it," I cut him off. "Have you told Jameson that you plan on playing him in this movie?"

"I'm going to," he hedges, but it's a safe bet that he's not. "You haven't told him, have you?"

"No. I've been trying to think of a way to break his heart even further. You know, his father was recently murdered, and the police are investigating him for the crime," I rattle off the facts in a flat voice.

"Wait," Levi says, taking a few steps closer to me. "If you're Hans's daughter..."

"Stepdaughter," I correct him. At the moment, that qualification feels pretty important. So does the fact that Levi isn't listening to a word that I say.

He whistles. "I'm a little surprised. I mean, I knew Hans was a kinky fucker, but..."

"Stop right there. I know about the sex scene."

"Don't you mean *scenes*? Personally, I'm all for

them. They're bringing Blake Lively in to test to play you." His mouth curls as if he's imagining her naked.

I groan, wondering how hard I have to hit my head against the stonework out here before I lose consciousness.

"Then again, Blake can't hold a candle to you." Levi takes another step toward me. This time, there's no hesitance in it.

I stare him down. "Keep your hands, and everything else, to yourself."

"I'd just like to know more about your side of the story." He brushes a finger down my bare shoulder, and I jump back.

"Here's a fun fact," I snap. "There's legitimately no part of that movie that's based in reality."

"That's because audiences don't want reality," Levi begins to explain.

Now I wish I'd let him go swimming after all. It would be a lot easier to drown him.

"Save the spin," I advise, "and get the hell out of here, before I tell the Wests why you really stopped in for a visit."

"It's a job. It's not personal."

"Do you really think they're going to feel that way?" I ask.

"I do."

"Then you're either stupid or you're lying to yourself. If you honestly believe they won't care, you should walk inside and tell them right now why you're here," I call his bluff.

"They've got a lot going on right now, and I wouldn't..."

"Yeah. That's what I thought," I mutter, ignoring his sorry excuse.

"Emma, you have to understand—"

"What's going on?" Jameson interrupts us. I don't have to look at my boyfriend to know that he's angry. Taking a mental step back, I evaluate the situation. Super-hot movie star friend standing way too close to current girlfriend, while he pleads with her. Yeah, this looks bad from any angle.

Levi comes to the same conclusion, because he backs away from me and holds up his hands in surrender. "It's not what it looks like, man."

"Really? Because it looks like you're hitting on my girlfriend."

"Is this the part where you two bump chests, and wrestle around on the ground?" I ask them. Jameson holds up a warning finger, but I slap it away.

"Have you still not figured out that I don't like to be told what to do?"

"And I don't like friends who overstep their bounds." As he moves in closer, I'm just starting to realize that this is about to come to blows.

"Look, man. I don't want to fight you. I have to be on set next week and..."

Jameson's fist finishes that sentence for him.

Levi grabs his nose, as blood begins to gush from it. "Did you just break my nose? Do you have any idea what this nose is worth?"

Jameson takes out his wallet and tosses a few hundred dollar bills at his feet. "That ought to cover it."

Turning toward me, he gestures towards the house. "Come inside."

I put my hands on my hips and shake my head. "I'm not taking your orders."

"Can we do this somewhere else?" Jameson suggests.

"No," I refuse, "because Levi has something to tell you."

"I do?" Levi adds in confusion.

Before he can work out that I'm forcing my hand to get him to confess, Jameson shoves him against the column. "Did you touch her? Did you lay a fucking hand on her?"

Levi shoves him away. "I don't want to hurt you."

"There's a difference between stage fighting and real fighting," Jameson warns him.

My stomach clenches in anticipation at his words. Maybe it's a little primeval of me to get off on watching two beautiful men make each other bleed, but if it's wrong, I don't want to be right.

"Tell him why you're here, Levi." I call out to

them, hoping they can hear it past the roar of adrenaline that's taken over their reasoning.

"What's going on out here?" Monroe steps onto the patio, her eyes flashing from her brother to Levi. "You didn't start a fist fight, did you?"

"*I* didn't," Jameson says with emphasis.

I can't keep it in any longer.

"Levi came here because he's going to play you in the biopic that Hans Von Essen is directing." The truth explodes from me. Not telling them would be as bad is lying. Something Levi might feel comfortable with, but I can't anymore.

"Is this true?" Jameson asks in a hollow voice.

Levi hesitates, which is answer enough.

"Get the fuck out," Jameson orders him. "And stay away. Don't call. Don't come by. Our lawyers will handle this."

"Lawyers?" Levi repeats. "I don't have a lawyer."

"Then I suggest you get one." Jameson turns his back towards his former friend.

"You can't sue me because I'm taking a role."

"Maybe not, but I can find something to sue you for, and I will."

Levi balks at Jameson's threat. "You wouldn't actually do that."

"A day ago, I might have said, 'You wouldn't actually take a role where you say I murdered my father.' I guess we're both full of surprises. Do you know how easy it would be for me to pull the plug on you playing this role?"

"I'd like to see you try," Levi sneers. It's the most unattractive he's ever looked, and for the first time I notice that his teeth are slightly crooked. One ear is larger than the other, and there's slight acne scars on his face. I guess a good smile can really disguise an asshole.

"Monroe, back me up." Levi addresses her and turns on the charm, but she simply raises an eyebrow.

"You heard what he said. Get out."

"I thought we were friends."

"We were," she informs him. "But this is about family."

"Your family's fucked up. You both know it. You both know how much your father hid. How he treated your mom. You told me so yourself."

"Yeah, it's a fucked up family," Jameson takes a step closer, and Levi flinches. "But it's our family, and you're not a part of it."

"What did I miss?" Hugo asks, rubbing his hands together as he steps outside.

Levi wipes his bloody nose with the back of his hand, and then straightens up. "Nothing. You didn't miss anything. I was just leaving."

"That's too bad," Hugo says, clapping him on the back as he passes, oblivious to the tension between the four of us. "Next time, I want to hear all about you getting up on Blake Lively."

Levi casts a glance toward Jameson. "Sure. I'll tell you all about it."

Then he walks into the house and out of our lives.

"How long have you known about this?" Jameson asks me when the others go into the house.

"Since the night we left Palm Springs. I'm sorry. I should have told you."

"No. Don't apologize to me, Duchess. You didn't do anything wrong."

"I didn't know how to tell you that your best friend betrayed you," I admit.

"I think it's hard for someone like you to understand."

"Understand what?" I whisper, as he moves in closer, his lips slanting towards mine.

"Disloyalty."

"I know a thing or two about it," I think of Becca and the lies she kept from me.

"Maybe you do, but there's not an ounce of it in your body. It's one of the reasons..."

Before he can finish the sentence, I kiss him, because I trust him, and he trusts me. Right now with our worlds as fucked up as they are, that has to count for something.

When we break apart, I'm panting. Jameson

presses his forehead against mine, lingering there despite the sweat from the heat of the evening.

"Can I stay with you for a while?"

"You can stay with me forever," he promises. Then, he seals that vow with a kiss.

Chapter 18

HIS MOM SHOWS me to a spare room. Obviously, things are a bit different when she's home. She smiles knowingly as she opens the closet and takes a guest robe out, laying it across the bed. She continues to point out where I can find towels, or shampoo, or a spare tooth brush.

"You didn't have to go to all this trouble," I say to her, when she asks if there's anything else I need.

"Nonsense, this is why we have guest rooms. Jameson mentioned that you're only seventeen. I don't feel comfortable allowing a seventeen-year-old to share a bed with her boyfriend."

I bite my lip, wondering why on earth I can't will the ground to open up and swallow me whole when I need it to.

"I knew your mother," she continues, "and I think she'd agree with me on this."

"You have no idea," I say under my breath. Of course, if it was up to her, I wouldn't be staying with the Wests; she'd be taking a restraining order out against them. I keep that to myself, though.

After she's left, I look around the large bedroom, feeling out of place. I creep quietly to the door when I hear voices in the hallway.

"You don't have to put us in separate rooms," Jameson says to her.

I hear her muffled laugh through the door. "I've seen how you look at her. It's for the best. There's enough police scrutiny on you at the moment. Keeping some distance between you and her is a good idea while she's still underage."

"I know, we've already talked about it."

"You have?" she says in surprise.

"We talk about a lot of things, Mom. She's not like other girls."

Those are the words we all long to hear because isn't every new boyfriend or girlfriend the same until one is different?

I'm different for Jameson.

The thought settles over me, sinking deep in my bones, and when I climb into the guest room bed, I drift away peacefully.

Sometime in the middle of the night, I'm awakened when he slips in beside me.

"You're not supposed to be in here," I murmur sleepily.

He spoons against me and presses a kiss to the back of my neck. "Try to keep me away, Duchess."

I wiggle closer to him, shamelessly pushing my ass against his groin.

"Duchess, what are you wearing?" he asks in a strangled voice.

"What I always wear to bed." It's harder to feign innocence when you're half asleep, but I do my best. "My panties and a tank top."

I already know what's gotten his attention. Ninety-nine percent of the time, I'm a boy shorts kind of girl, but since I'd had to wear that teeny tiny romper today, I'd opted for a thong. His hand skims over my bare ass cheek, and he groans.

"You're the one who wants to wait," I remind him.

"Shh," he hushes me. "I'm trying really hard to remember why." I giggle, enjoying the feel of his hands roaming all over me. "My mom is down the hall, remember?"

I flip over to face him, tucking my head against his shoulder. "I don't think she'll hear us."

"Duchess, if I have anything to say about it, they'll hear you in China," he promises. Then he kisses me on the forehead. "You're just going to have to wait."

"It would be easier if you didn't keep getting into bed with me," I tell him.

"It would be easier if you weren't half naked."

He sighs deeply and moves his palms upward until they're resting on the small of my back. "Stop pouting."

"It's dark, how do you know I'm pouting?"

"You're pouting so loudly that I can hear it. Get some sleep," he advises me.

"Won't we get in trouble if she catches you in here?"

"Yeah," he says wearily. "She'll slap me on the wrist and then ask if I want breakfast."

"I wish my mom was like yours."

"Be careful what you wish for," he says mysteriously. I'm not certain what to make of that statement, so I let it slide. Every moment I've experienced with Evelyn West leads me to believe that she has a wonderful relationship with her children. Then again, it took her days to return home after her husband was murdered. She claimed her father was sick but if my own life proves anything, it's that appearances can be deceiving.

"I don't want to sleep," I admit to Jameson. "I have too many nightmares."

"I won't let you have any tonight." His arms tighten around my waist. "Tonight you're only going to have good dreams. What do you want to dream about, Duchess?"

"My birthday," I say shyly.

"Why? Is there something you're looking forward to?" I can hear the smile in his voice.

"I have a feeling it's going to be the best birthday ever."

"If I have anything to say about it, it will be." He keeps his lips pressed to my forehead, whispering the words across my bare skin. They tingle across my scalp and race down my neck, settling low in my belly. "Have you thought any more about where you want to go?"

"Nowhere too far," I tell him.

"Paris and London are out?"

"Too far. I want to get there as quickly as possible," I admit.

"What about Mexico? There's this little resort in Playa del Carmen. We can sleep near the water."

"Sleep?" I repeat.

"Miss Southerly, what are you suggesting?" He says, in mock horror.

"It'd be easier for me to give you a preview," I murmur. Then I move my lips to his.

"I SHOULD HAVE KNOWN you'd be in here." Waking up to Monroe's smug voice is not my idea of a good morning. I burrow down into the covers, leaving Jameson to deal with his sister.

"What do you want, Monroe?" he mutters, rolling away from me and then instantly falling back to sleep. For a second, I'm reminded of how things used to be with Becca.

"You two have company."

"What time is it?" I whisper over his snores.

"Eight."

Monroe strikes me as the type to get up at the break of dawn to do two hours of cardio. When I sit up, my suspicions are confirmed when I see she's in a sports bra and shorts.

"Who is it?" I ask, praying it's not my dad.

There's no smugness in her tone when she says, "Detective Mackey."

She might as well have shot me up with espresso. I jump out of bed and shrug on the robe her mom left me.

"Don't wake him up," I order her.

She grabs my arm, digging her nails into my skin. "What are you hiding?"

"Nothing." I yank free of her grip. "In case you missed it, your brother doesn't always act rationally when he thinks I'm in trouble."

I take the stairs slowly. I'm not exactly excited for my reunion with my favorite federal investigator. The fact that she's here as early as is socially acceptable is a pretty good indicator that she's bringing bad news with her. It occurs to me too late that I should have asked Monroe for more details. Had Mackey come to see both Jameson and me? Or just him?

Or me?

When I reach the sitting room, I can't help but

notice that the slick bob she'd sported when she came to town is a bit too long. She's been working overtime. I might feel sorry for her except for the fact that she's trying to put my boyfriend away for murder.

"Can I get you some coffee?" I ask.

Channel your inner hostess much, Emma. I don't even know where the coffeemaker is.

Mackey raises one eyebrow that's in serious need of intervention. "Making yourself at home, aren't you?"

I stopped fidgeting and sit up straighter.

"I'm attempting to be polite, you should try it."

There's a hint of a smile at her lips, but she doesn't give me the satisfaction. She leans back and crosses her legs, regarding me for a long moment before she comes to the point. "There's going to be a press conference today. I felt you should know."

"I had no idea that interest in the case has waned so much that you have to solicit attention door-to-door," I say with a shrug. If she's going to pretend that she doesn't find me amusing then I'll pretend that I don't find her or her games interesting.

She folds her hands in her lap. "Would you like to know what it's going to be about?"

"I'm assuming the murderer. Are you trying to tell me you've done some genuine police work and have a real suspect finally?"

"Yes, we do." Mackey tilts her head and meets my eyes. "You."

I don't blink. Partially because I don't want her to see that she's spooked me, but mostly because I'm frozen. I force myself to respond. "You really are desperate."

"Says the girl playing house at a billionaire's."

"Fine, I'll bite." I lean forward, placing my elbows on my knees to close some of the distance between us. "What do you have on me?"

"First, can I ask you a couple of questions?"

"Should I have a lawyer present?" I counter. If I'm smart I'll kick her out, but curiosity has gotten the better of me.

"You should," Jameson says from the doorway. There's no sign that he's been sleeping. He's dressed and alert while I can claim neither thing. Not bothering to look my way, he prowls into the room with his eyes trained on her.

"Mr. West, how lovely to see you." Mackey sounds anything but pleased that he's joined us. "I'm having a private conversation with your girlfriend."

"Anything you can say to her, you can say in front of me."

It's a line right out of a CSI episode.

"Is that true?" she asks me.

"Yeah," I say without hesitation. "I don't keep anything from him."

"So young to have so little secrets. How long have you two known each other?"

"Long enough," Jameson answers for me while I do the math. Has it really been less than two months? "Do you have actual questions? And can they wait for my lawyers to arrive?"

"You don't need a lawyer," Mackey corrects him. "She does."

"I misspoke. I meant *our* lawyers."

"You two have gotten close. It's surprising given that you've known each other such a short time—or did you know each other before?" she asks.

I groan and slouch back in my chair. Apparently, Mackey will be playing the role of good cop *and* bad cop today. It's hard to believe anyone actually falls for this crap, but pitting couples against one another must work if she's trying it.

"I waive my right to an attorney."

"Emma, I wouldn't advise that," Jameson begins, but I hold up a hand.

"Look, I don't feel like waiting around all day to get to the point. Let her ask her questions. We know the truth, so let's see what she believes is so rock solid that she's here accusing me of murder."

"Right now it's only gut," Mackey admits.

"You want me to be the one who killed him. Should I be flattered or offended?"

She doesn't answer my question. "You make the most sense."

"Enough theorizing," Jameson intercedes. "Ask your questions and get out."

"According to your statement, you were present at the West Casino on the night Nathaniel West was murdered." She takes a notepad from her purse and flips it open.

"Yes, and that's still true," I promise her. "The darn time machine I've been constructing isn't finished yet, so I haven't been able to change history."

She continues, ignoring my sarcasm. I guess my mom is right that my dark sense of humor isn't my friend.

"Furthermore, you claimed that that the two of you were together the entire evening."

"None of these are questions," Jameson points out.

"No," I respond, eager to get this over with so that I can separate the two of them. "I told you that we went skinning dipping, we spent some time together, and we fell asleep."

Her eyes narrow. So much for trying to call my bluff. What would be the point of trying to change my story now?

"Are you certain that's what happened?"

What do they say? The truth will set you free. Or you'll just get asked the same question over and over until you lie simply to break the cycle. "Yes, that's exactly what happened."

Jameson asked me not to lie on his behalf, which is why I don't bother to claim he was actually next to me the entire evening.

"So, either of you could have gotten up in your sleep, and the other one wouldn't have known." She's having a hard time asking actual questions. I guess it's a good thing that she's sticking to the law and not the order side. Leading the witness, anyone?

"I suppose." I grant her this one tiny admission, mostly because it's pretty fucking obvious.

"Who exactly do you think did it now, Detective Mackey?" Jameson cuts straight to the point. "Because without evidence, this is becoming harassment."

"Isn't it wonderful that the Federal Bureau of Investigation is above such petty concerns?" She smiles serenely at him before turning her attention back to me. "Emma, are you a virgin?"

I snort in surprise. Of all the things Detective Mackey could be here to ask me, that's pretty far down on the list of possibilities.

"You don't have to answer that," Jameson says, but she holds up a hand to silence him once more.

"Miss Southerly wants to be cooperative."

Challenge accepted. "No, I am not."

"How long have you been sexually active?" she continues.

"I'm sorry, but what does this have to do with the murder?" I bypass her question because my answer is pretty embarrassing, especially when you consider I've been practically begging my boyfriend to screw me all week.

"I'd prefer if you would just answer the question."

"Fine." I cross my arms over my chest as if that can shield me from the oncoming humiliation. "I lost my virginity a couple of years ago in a rash moment of stupidity, and I haven't done it since then."

"So you aren't sexually active?"

It's strange to see Mackey unnerved. It isn't the response she expected, but I'm still not certain what this has to do with Nathaniel West or what happened that night.

"No, I'm not having sex if that answers your question."

"You'll pardon me if I find that surprising." She scribbles a note on her pad of paper.

"You mean: how did I land a billionaire without the aid of my vagina?" I retort. If I have to be uncomfortable, so does everybody. "Look, have me go to a doctor or something. It's probably been so long that it's closed back up."

"Vaginas don't close back up."

"Gee, thanks for the biology lesson," I tell her, "but these are the facts. I haven't had sex in over three years."

"So now that she's answered your question,

would you care to elaborate on exactly what you were hoping to find out today?" Jameson asks.

She closes the notepad and shoves it inside her bag. "She's given me an answer, whether or not it proves to be true is another matter entirely."

Oh my god. Where is a wall to hit when you need one?

"If I had information to share with you, I would." I'm tired of the games and double speak, so I opt for being direct. "But I don't lie, and I don't appreciate people who show up and accuse me of doing so."

"Noted." Mackey stands up and smooths down her pants. "We'll be in touch if we have further questions."

"I'll be holding my breath," I promise her.

"Exactly what did any of this have to do with my father's murder?" Jameson asks as he shows her to the front door

"Well, since you two are so innocent, you can find out when everyone else does. Press conference is at noon."

I hate to admit it, but we both know we'll be watching.

Chapter 19

JAMESON TAKES me by the hand and leads me towards the stairs as soon as she's gone. We should talk or come up with a plan, but I can't find the energy to do either.

"I can't go back to sleep," I warn him.

"Can I have a moment with Emma?" Evelyn asks, stepping out of the shadows before we reach the stairwell. Jameson considers for a moment, but his mom must be on the pre-approved list because he excuses himself.

"I'll be waiting in your room," he says, before he leaves me with her.

Dark circles rim Evelyn's eyes. Is anyone in this house getting sleep?

"What did they want?" she asks when we're alone.

"To accuse me of murdering your husband," I

blurt out. "I might as well tell you now because there's going to be a press conference."

I don't know how I expect her to react, but she surprises me by wrapping me in a tight hug.

"How can you know that I…" I let the thought trail away.

She steps back, her hands gripping my shoulders. "The same way I know Jamie is innocent."

"He's your son." It seems like an obvious fact to point out.

"He is, and he's in love with you. As far as I'm concerned that makes you my daughter and I know what my children are capable of."

I swallow hard, wishing I deserved her faith in me. If she knew the secrets I'm hiding, she wouldn't think so highly of me.

"Get some rest."

When I step into my room, Jameson closes the door behind us then he takes me in his arms.

"Mackey won't touch you," he vows.

"I don't understand why she was asking all those questions," I admit. "Jameson, you have to know that I had nothing to do—"

"I already know that, Duchess. I'm going to draw you a bath and then I'm going to go downstairs and get on the phone with my lawyer."

"You don't have to do that." He stops me with a kiss.

"Yes I do."

I blink against the prickly heat of tears. "She's going to try to turn us against one another."

"She's going to fail," he promises me.

"There's going to be interrogations, maybe even a trial." I'm too panicked to let him reassure me, but he grabs my chin in his hands and directs my gaze to his.

"I'm not going to let that happen, Emma"

"I don't have the resources you have unless I ask Hans for help," I rattle on.

"You have every resource at my disposal," he corrects me.

"They're going to make you go in there and talk about our sex life." *Or lack thereof*, I add silently.

He pauses and I see the wheels turning behind his blue eyes. "There's a way around that."

"How?" I plead. I need to know how he can fix this. I want to believe he can because for the first time since this started, I'm truly scared.

"You'll be eighteen soon." He doesn't have to remind me, it's all I've been thinking about. "Emma, they can't force you to testify against your spouse."

I jerk away as if he'd suddenly announced he has a contagious disease. "What?"

"Spousal privilege. If it comes to it, we can get married." His words are detached. He's suggesting a preemptive strike.

Call me old-fashioned, I'm not walking down the aisle as a strategic move. "We are not getting married." Disbelief mixes with fear. "We haven't even had sex yet, how are we having this conversation? I still have a year of high school and I'm pretty sure I don't want to spend it labelled as the gold-digger murderess."

"You're neither of those things," he reprimands me.

"Tell that to the rest of my graduating class," I grumble.

"Who cares what they think?"

Apparently I do. I'm too shocked over this moment of self-discovery to share it.

"Look, I'm not going to make you marry me," Jameson begins.

"Good because I'm not."

"I have to admit that I'm offended that you don't want to."

"It's not that..." I search for the right words to explain the crazy jumble of thoughts in my head. How on earth did things get this screwed up? I spent the better part of the last week begging him to take me to bed. Now he's offering to put a ring on it. Everything about this scenario is backwards. "You don't have to do something this extreme."

In the end, I opt to spare his feelings.

"It's not a big deal."

"It is a big deal." I don't bother to hide my

incredulousness. "Marriage is a very big deal. At least it is to me."

"You have to remember I was raised by a billionaire. Jesus, I can afford to have a few wives."

"A few wives, huh?" My eyes narrow at the thought of someone else catching Jameson's attention.

"You look jealous, Duchess." I can hear how pleased he sounds.

"Don't worry about me. Continue to visualize your trophy wife collection. Might I suggest mahogany for the cabinet you keep them in?"

"You are jealous." He grabs the sash of my robe and tugs me closer. "I like jealous on you."

"I don't." How he's managed to distract me from the drama at hand is beyond me.

Jameson goes into the ensuite bathroom and begins to run water in the bathtub.

"I'm only going to be downstairs," he says as I slip off my clothes and grab a towel, waiting for the tub to finish filling up.

When he reaches the bathroom door, I call after him, "By the way, that was the worst marriage proposal of all time."

He pokes his head back in the door. "I'll do better next time."

What have I gotten myself into?

When the tub is nearly full, I turn off the tap. I'm about to get in when there's a knock on the bathroom door. I wrap my towel around me. Jameson wouldn't bother to knock, especially if there was a possibility of catching a glimpse of the goods. I expect to see Evelyn on the other side of the door, but it's Monroe. "I brought you this."

She offers me a glass of water before she opens her palm to reveal a small blue pill.

"Umm." I hesitate. I'm not exactly in the habit of taking drugs from strangers, not that Monroe is a stranger exactly. She's something worse: an enemy. Although, in the last few days, she seems to be heading into neutral territory.

"Xanax," she assures me. "I overheard what Mackey had to say."

"You can't tell anyone..." I say in a rush.

There's a struggle in her crystal blue eyes, but after a moment she says, "I'm not going to, Emma. I know you didn't do it."

I want to ask her how she knows and where her sudden suspicious faith has come from. Instead, I take the pill from her and pop it in my mouth.

"Try to relax," she advises me. "Jameson is already on the phone with the lawyers."

I swallow a gulp of water and hand her the glass. "Thank you."

It's hard for me to get it out, and, judging by the way she flinches, it's hard for her to accept my gratitude. Which is why I can't let this go.

"Why are you being so nice to me?" I ask her.

She shrugs. "You're a guest, and well...I get the impression you're not going anywhere."

"I'm not," I warn her.

"Then I guess we have to get used to each other." It's a mediocre truce at best. One we've been forced into, rather than chosen on our own, but it's a start.

"Need anything else?" she asks. I shake my head no, still too dumbfounded by her sudden generous spirit.

The Wests certainly know how to surprise you, I think as I sink into the bathtub.

"It's a good thing," I say to myself even as I wonder what curve ball they'll throw at me next.

"I don't understand why her parents don't take care of this."

I freeze outside the kitchen, waiting for Monroe to say more. I expect Jameson to defend me, but it's his mother who comes to my rescue.

"Not every family has the resources to cope with a scandal of this magnitude."

Scandal. I'm a scandal. And they're sitting around trying to figure out how to handle me.

"Her stepfather has money," Monroe points out.

"I won't allow it," Jameson informs them. There's a finality in his tone that leaves no room for questioning.

This impromptu family meeting is none of my

business—except that it's obvious they're talking about me.

Jameson continues, finally shifting the topic away from his ill-begotten girlfriend. "I spoke with Richard yesterday. A number of new suits have been filed against the corporation."

"Fucking vultures." Monroe doesn't mince words.

"Watch your language," her mother chastises her.

"It's true," Monroe defends herself. "A man is dead, so why not try to bleed his assets dry."

"What can we do about it?" Evelyn asks. "Or do we do anything?"

"It could destroy most of our holdings," Jameson advises her.

"But we'd be fine?"

"Yes." He clears his throat, and I wish I could see his face. "But the people we employ won't be."

"Sometimes I forget how different you are from your father," she says softly.

"That's why I've decided to step in as interim CEO," he announces.

I gasp loudly enough that everyone in the other room falls silent. Next time I'll wear bells so they can hear me coming. Steeling myself, I wander into the kitchen.

Jameson shakes his head, not buying my casual

entrance for a second. "Care to join in our family meeting, Duchess?"

"I'm not family," I say dismissively. "I thought I'd see about some coffee."

"Nonsense," Evelyn pipes up. "Sit down. These topics concern you. I'll get you some coffee."

I head towards the bar stool at the far end, but Monroe moves to it, allowing me to sit next to Jameson. I try to hide my surprise at the thoughtful gesture, but it's like I'm in the Twilight Zone.

"Catch Emma up." Evelyn hands me a mug. I cup it with both hands, savoring the warm ceramic against my palms. Jameson gives me a rundown of what they discussed. I can't bring myself to tell him that I overheard most of it already.

"That brings us back to the fact that I'm stepping in as CEO." His gaze locks with mine, and he waits for me to speak.

"Okay," I say, wondering if he wants more input or if he's torturing me for acting like I haven't already overheard all of this. But I'm less concerned with the fact that I've been caught eavesdropping. "Is that what you want?"

"That's a really good question," his mother backs me up. "You left business school."

"I don't know," he admits after a long pause, "but it is my responsibility."

I want to tell him to screw responsibility. He owes his father, and the legacy he left behind him, nothing. But sitting in this small circle, I realize that he's not doing it for himself. Risking the company's assets undermines his family's financial stability.

Isn't that the reason I'd stuck around the pawn shop for so long? The burdens we carry for those we love are the heaviest and hardest to release.

"Emma?" He wants my opinion and for a split second it's as if we're the only two people in the room.

"I'm with you," I reassure him. "Do what you have to."

"Then for the time being I'll take over."

Evelyn's eyes flick to mine and I catch a flash of approval that she quickly masks. That's when it hits me that she wants Jameson to step in. So why did she remind him that he'd abandoned business school?

I clear my throat awkwardly. Despite my initial reservations—and a lifetime of being spoon-fed a hatred of the West family—I can't take advantage of their kindness, even Monroe's begrudging civility. When I have their attention, I begin, "I overheard. I don't need help with lawyers."

"Like hell you don't," Jameson growls and all three of our heads swivel in his direction.

"Down, boy," Monroe orders him.

Jameson glowers at her, his face a stony mask that conceals a raging storm of emotions I can only sense. "You don't know everything. The situation…"

"Sucks," Monroe finishes for him. "But don't let Jamie fool you. We won't know much until the press conference."

"Except that scoop from the DA's office," he reminds her.

"What scoop?" I do my best to ignore the fifties slang term.

"They're leaving some information out during the press release today," Monroe says.

"I bet it won't be anything important," I grumble.

That's why Mackey came by—to watch me squirm. If she only knew that she'd left too soon.

"We should know what it is in a few days," Jameson tells me.

Pressing my lips together, I allow this to sink in. "How are we going to find out?"

"Do you want the truth or plausible deniability?"

"On second thought, I don't need to know." The West's money could buy any information he wants, and there's no way to talk him into leaving this case alone.

At noon, we gather in the rec room and turn on the local news channel. We don't have to wait long before the district attorney appears at the podium. Mackey takes her place beside them and they wait for the crowd to quiet.

"New evidence has been found in the investigation of one of Belle Mère's most prominent citizens…"

I dare a glance around the room. Nathaniel West's family wasn't invited onto that stage for this announcement. Not only is the FBI keeping the Wests out of the spotlight, they've already drawn their conclusions.

Jameson grabs my hand and squeezes it tightly as the DA hands the mic over to Detective Mackey.

"After extensive examination of Mr. West's body, investigators discovered trace DNA. A follow-up search of the crime scene produced an object with both Mr. West's DNA and that of an unidentified source. Due to the nature of the evidence, our team has concluded that the victim had participated in sexual intercourse on the night of his death—"

Jameson turns off the television. "I'm sorry, Mom."

"Ignoring it won't make it untrue." The exhaustion in her voice is at odds with the cheerful attitude she turns on for most customers.

"That's why she came here." I clap my hand over my mouth. Detective Mackey assumes I had sex with Mr. West.

"At least we know what we're dealing with," Jameson says grimly.

"Most of it," I grumble.

Evelyn pushes onto her feet and glances around

the room, unable to make eye contact. "I'm going to lie down."

No one makes a move to stop her and as soon as she's out of earshot, I turn on Jameson and Monroe. "Did she know your dad was a…"

"Cheater?" Jameson fills in the blank. "Everyone knew."

I glance in the direction she fled. "She seemed so surprised."

"Humiliated," Monroe clarifies.

It's one thing to have an unfaithful spouse and another to have your family's dirty laundry hung out to dry for the whole town to see. When she doesn't emerge from her room for dinner, I begin to worry.

"Should we check on her?" I ask Jameson.

"This isn't her first rodeo," Monroe jumps in. "She needs time."

I decide that she also needs tea. One of the few comforting memories I have of my own mom involves hot tea. She'd brew it when we had stomach bugs or colds. Other times she made it for no reason at all. I dig through the cupboards looking for teabags. When Jameson asks what I'm doing, he stays out of my way. Monroe, on the other hand, helps me raid the pantry.

She holds a box of tea bags triumphantly.

"It's herbal." She scrunches up her nose like decaffeinated is below her.

"Do you know how she takes it?" I ask. In the

end, I set off to her room with a cup of tea sans milk or sugar. Knocking lightly, I wait until I hear a faint *come in*.

"I brought you some tea." I place the cup on her nightstand.

"I'm sorry that you're mixed up in this."

"I mixed myself up." I could have said no to Josie that night and stayed home. I could have blended into the party. I could have never met Jameson. All the fear and heartbreak is worth it, knowing that he's in my life.

She lowers her voice to a whisper that I have to lean to hear, "There are very few people in Belle Mère that you can trust. Jameson is one of them."

I don't point out that he's the only West on her list. I read between the lines instead.

Chapter 20

LIFE FALLS into a rhythm that's steady but building in intensity. Hopeful reporters hover at the end of the family's private drive. A handful of friends finagle invitations to sit by the grotto's pool. Television networks negotiate private interviews.

When I answer the door early one morning, I'm stupid enough to accept a package.

"Don't!" Jameson calls out but it's already in my hands. He snatches it away. Inside, there's a subpoena for me to appear at a medical clinic by the end of the week.

"I don't understand." I study the letter like it's written in ancient greek, but he's on the phone to his lawyers. He talks to them so often that we should ask them to move in.

They want your blood, he mouths before his call connects.

My life has become a game of playing house with a billionaire's toys all while under a microscope. If I'm not careful, whoever holds that lens might use it to set me on fire.

By the end of the week this is my new normal, and I hate it. The only positive in this whole nightmare is when Jameson appears at the breakfast table in a three-piece suit and tie.

I whistle when he comes into the room.

"Doesn't he clean up nicely?" Evelyn reaches out to ruffle his hair but he sidesteps her.

"Duchess, a word?"

I hurry after him, but when I round the corner to the living room, he sweeps me off my feet. I grip his tie as he kisses me deeply.

"Mr. West," I say breathlessly when we break apart.

"Mr. West was my father," he says in a tight voice.

"And now it's you," I whisper, straightening the knot of his tie. I bite my lip, and he groans.

"If you keep it up, I'll never make it out of here," he warns in a dark voice.

That's exactly what I want. I didn't know Nathaniel West. I grew up conditioned to be prejudiced against him. The more I learn now, the less I want to know. Something about Jameson willingly taking up his place, even if only in the family business, makes me uneasy.

"I want you to keep Maddox with you today."

"That almost sounds like a request," I murmur with approval.

The muscles in his jaw clench before he admits, "It is."

"I don't need a babysitter," I remind him.

"The reporters will—"

"Let me worry about that. We had an arrangement," I cut him off before he can renege on our agreement that Maddox is at *my* disposal. Brushing a renegade copper strand from his forehead, I continue, "Go play with your billions."

"Yes," he says dryly. "I think my first order of business will be building a large vault filled with gold coins that I can dive into Scrooge McDuck style."

"I'm sure the board will approve."

He chuckles, but there's a nervous edge to his laughter. When he finally lowers me to my feet, he pauses with his hands on my waist. "I love you."

"I love you, too." With the whole world burning around us, it's amazing that those three little words nearly knock me off my feet every time he says them.

"Give Maddox a chance, and stay safe." It's not a request, it's an order. I salute him before I push him towards the front door. He steals one final kiss before he climbs into the back of a chauffeured sedan.

Getting out of the house without being hounded by wannabe reporters looking to score their big break is the real trick. The driver will deliver him to the West Corporation headquarters. I have no clue how I'll get by them. I dress in a black wrap dress, pinning my hair low on my neck. No make-up or lipstick. As much as possible, I need to blend in. I head towards my Mercedes, which has been parked in the driveway since Jameson had someone retrieve it from the desert.

Maddox appears as soon as I touch the handle.

"Can I drive you somewhere?" he asks.

I whirl around and give him a wicked smile. "No, but here's what you're going to do."

THE ONE BENEFIT of staying locked up for a week is that it's pretty easy to trick the reporters waiting on the other side. I send Maddox ahead of me, along with one of the Wests's house maids who needed to run some errands. When I reach the gate at the end of the private drive, there's nary a leach insight.

No one's seen this car, so I put as much distance between me and the West residence as possible before I begin to slow down. I double-check my rearview mirrors and turn left a bunch of times until I'm satisfied that no one is following me. Who knew you could learn how to lose a tail online? Thanks Google.

It's strange how different it feels when I pull up to the boxy, two bedroom house that's only a few blocks away. The stark difference in Jameson's reality and my past can't be denied. But even as my stomach begins to churn from nerves, taking the walkway to the front door feels like coming home.

I nearly give up when no one answers after I knock twice. I have a key, but I can't shake how angry Josie had been when I'd touched her phone last week. How would she feel if I walked into her house? I stand there for a moment, staring at the locked door between us until it opens.

"Emma!" Marion tugs her robe tightly around her.

"I'm sorry!' I stare at her in wide-eyed horror as I realize how early it is at the Deckard house. She probably just got off work a few hours ago.

But Marion waves off my apology. "It's my day off. I'd invite you in, but Josie has the flu."

"How is she?" I ask.

"She's fine. Probably something she ate."

I want to know about more than her stomach cramps, but I don't push the topic. Marion Deckard didn't invite me into her house, which means Josie's either really sick or she doesn't want to see me.

"Tell her I stopped by?"

"Of course," she promises, her eyes darting around the street before she steps back inside.

Maybe they both would prefer not to see me.

I don't have time to throw myself a pity party. If misery loves company, it hates productivity. My time is running out. According to the court, I have to appear at the clinic by Monday. That gives me the weekend to piece together the bizarre trail of clues The Dealer left behind for us. His posts have become less frequent. I don't know what that means, but I'm not going to miss my opportunity to figure out what he's trying to tell me.

As if to back up that decision, a new photo appears on his feed in the late morning. It's from last week. I'm in the black romper walking into a nondescript office building. I know what that place is and I know what he's trying to tell me.

I have an appointment that I need to keep this evening. But first, I have time to make a house call.

Dominic Chamber's office is a reporter-free zone, so he must have upheld his word that no one would know he's been working for me. It's early enough in the day that he's at his desk. The creeps come out at night in this city.

He glances up from his computer and exhales when he makes eye contact. Pushing away from the desk, he gestures for me to take an empty chair before he lounges in his own seat. "You're a hard woman to reach."

"I've been a little more cautious with blocked callers. Next time go through the Belle Mère police. They seem to know where I am at all hours."

He frowns. Maybe I'm not as funny as I think I am. "I called from several numbers."

"Sorry, but my lawyer"—it still feels ridiculous to say that—"made me block unknown callers."

"Understandable, given the circumstances. However, if we're going to continue to work together, I'll need a way to reach you. Get yourself a prepaid cell phone to use as a burner."

"A burner?" I repeat. I thought those were only for spy movies, but he nods seriously.

"Done," I promise him. "So if you've been trying to reach me, does that mean you have something?"

He shuffles a few folders around on his desk before he finds the one he wants. I could probably pay him in secretarial services.

"There's no record of who your sister's father is." Before I can thank him for his lackluster bit of news, he goes on, "In fact, most of her medical records and vital statistics have been sealed."

"What do you mean by sealed?"

"It's not so much that her father is unknown. It's more that he's hidden. Well, I might add."

"Why would they do that?" I ask. None of this makes sense. It had been hard enough to process that we had different fathers, but hearing the lengths my parents have gone to in order to bury that information is inconceivable.

"I asked myself the same question, so I started doing a little digging. I looked for your parents' names in conjunction with other legal proceedings. Adoption records, court records."

"Did you find anything?"

"Were you aware that your family accepted a large settlement from Nathaniel West about thirteen years ago?" he asks.

I nod. "My dad sued him in civil court for cutting him out of the business they started."

My parents used the funds as seed money to start Pawnography in an attempt to recapture the American dream he'd lost to his business partner.

Dominic rubs his temples. It's not the answer he's hoping for. "That's all I have so far. It's not much."

I can't help but think it's a lot more than he thinks. Someone has gone to an awful lot of trouble to keep this quiet.

"How much do I owe you?" I ask him, taking my wallet from my purse.

Dominic holds up a chubby hand. "Nothing today. I haven't gotten the information you asked for."

"But you've been working on it," I say slowly.

"I'll be happy to bill you when I've figured this out."

I had no idea private investigators came with a satisfaction guarantee. Then again, considering his hourly billing rate, I deserve more answers.

"I'll be in touch," he promises.

I leave his office with more questions than answers. My mind churns through an endless stream of theories, many so ridiculous that I actually laugh at myself. I'm so distracted that I don't bother to check my surroundings when I exit his building. When I remember, I glance around, checking every angle. There's no one in sight.

Apparently being investigated for murder makes one both reckless and cautious.

As if he can read my thoughts, Jameson calls.

"World's best girlfriend," I answer glibly.

"Where are you, Duchess?" he asks in a lowered voice that's so deep that I get goosebumps.

"Running errands." It's not a lie technically.

"Without your bodyguard?" he guesses.

"Are you asking or do you know?"

"I know. Maddox called to tell me you had him running the maid to the grocery store," he says.

"We're out of eggs."

He pauses and I brace myself for a lecture. "Just promise me that you're being careful."

"I am. Look there's no safer place to be than on a suspect list." Whoever is framing me wants me alive. I could run around Vegas naked with my hair on fire and no one would touch me.

"Will I see you tonight?" he asks.

"You'll see me every night," I reassure him before we hang up. He'll see me tonight, but I have a very important date to keep first.

Chapter 21

LIES ARE SO easy to tell, but sins are so hard to forgive. It's odd how even something as simple as a coat of paint can be deceptive until viewed in the right light. I never knew what I preferred—a pretty lie or a sorry sinner—until now.

They've redone the lobby of the West Casino. I suppose if I ran a hotel that had seen a murder and an accident in less than two months, I might try to freshen up the joint, too.

It's a bit early to check-in, but as I get closer to my appointment with May from Cachè—and her secret identity—I get more nervous. I'd planned to ask Josie to come with me tonight. I'd never even gotten the chance to tell her about the plan before our falling out.

Before I reach the check-in counter, Mackey steps into my path. I halt, looking around to see if she's alone. I don't spot any other officers, but they are trained to blend in. It's good to see my tax dollars at work.

So much for flying under the radar.

"Are you here to arrest me?" I ask her directly.

"I'm here to talk to you *alone.*"

Translation: she wants to speak to me without Jameson or lawyers.

"I have lunch plans," I lie to her, "so this can't take too long."

She glances at the gold watch on her wrist. "Late lunch."

"Early interrogation," I counter. "I have until Monday to comply with the subpoena orders."

"You do," she confirms. "Let's grab a seat."

"Let's stand." I'm not about to let her get comfortable.

"Your boyfriend is calling in every favor in town to find out more about the DNA evidence we've uncovered."

I shrug. She wants me to bite, which is something I can do. "I keep telling him to watch less CSI. Next thing you'll know he'll be doing blood spatter analysis."

"We found a towel in the residence containing seminal residue…"

I do my best not to gag.

"And blood—as well as some tissue."

"Tissue?" I repeat, hoping she's talking about Kleenex.

"Preliminary reports suggest it's hymenal."

Some things you can't unhear. "Are you saying that Nathaniel West…"

"Had sexual intercourse with a woman we believe was a virgin at the time."

"Then there you go," I tell her. "That clears me because I'm not eligible for a white wedding."

"Given your intriguing sexual history, it's possible it could be you."

"I already told you that I'm not a virgin," I whisper furiously as a group of Japanese tourists roll past.

"According to your statement, you've only had sexual intercourse once. It's very likely that your hy—"

"Enough theories revolving around my vagina. None of this explains why you think it's me." I'm not a lawyer but there has to be some evidence actually linking me to the crime before they can start stealing my blood.

"That's why I'm here," she says. "I'm about to tell you what your boyfriend so desperately wants to know."

"Out of the goodness of your heart?"

"Before it's too late." It's not the answer I'm expecting. "Our investigations have discovered some interesting connections between your family and the Wests."

That hardly counts as brilliant detective work. "Everyone knows that our fathers hated one another."

"But why?" she asks. "It took some time to convince the court to unseal the documents, but we have our answer. Nathaniel West settled a civil suit with your father a number of years ago."

"I know. They had a disagreement about a business arrangement."

Mackey casts a wan smile at me and my heart skips a beat. "The matter was tried in a civil court, and the records were sealed to protect a minor."

In the middle of one of the busiest hotel lobbies in Las Vegas, the world stops.

"Did you know Nathaniel West was your sister's father?"

No seems like a grossly inadequate word.

Mackey continues, granting me no time to come to grips with this. "Both sets of DNA found at the murder scene were a partial match."

"I don't understand," I say slowly.

"One set belonged to Nathaniel West. The other belonged to his progeny."

MACKEY DOESN'T FOLLOW me when I run for the

lobby's bathroom. Progeny. Child. Daughter. The words assault me as I wretch over the toilet. If Becca was his daughter, of course, Mackey suspects I am, too.

I'm not, but someone else is. It can't be Monroe. She'd given the entire freshman class a front row seat to her debauchery. I know it isn't me.

At least, I know I'm not the one who…

I throw up again just considering what she told me. I might not be the one she's looking for, but I can't ignore the other bombshell she's dropped.

Becca was Nathaniel West's daughter, a fact both my parents knew—parents who've been desperate to break up my relationship with my boyfriend.

I vomit until I'm dry heaving stomach acid in the public restroom of a five-star resort. If Mackey wanted to be certain I'll submit to that DNA test, she knew exactly what button to push.

When I finally gather my strength, I rinse out my mouth in the sink. I can't bring myself to look in the mirror. I'm too afraid I'll find Nathaniel West staring back at me.

I check in to my room, ignoring the annoying cheerfulness of the front desk attendant. The hotel room has been redone to have a sleek, modern appeal. Everything is white and minimal with clean lines and the most abstract of abstract art, but the stale scent of cigarette smoke still hangs in the room. It's proof that Vegas is a city out of time, or maybe just one unhinged from reality. If it weren't for the acrid smell assaulting my nostrils, the space might actually seem luxurious. No doubt the renovation had been a ploy to try to convince visitors that the hotel is worth the hefty price tag.

Next month, I'll have some serious explaining to do when my mom and Hans get my emergency credit card bill. But if this situation doesn't count as a crisis, nothing ever will.

I sit on the edge of the bed and wait with my hands folded in my lap. Being nervous is strange. Of course, I've never called a service before. Until a few days ago, my only contact with call girls had been on the flyers littering the streets. Somehow it still feels inevitable. I'm in too deep not to follow the clues.

But *this* room in *this* hotel in *this* city could never hope to be more than a mirage. Because the one thing tourists never see is the truth. The bones of Las Vegas are rotten, weakened by greed and excess. Even in a fancy hotel room I can't see past that fact.

Just like I can't see past the fact that my whole life is a lie. Is it possible this should be my birthright?

Because I don't want it. Any of it. If what Mackey told me is true, she's stolen the only good thing in my life.

Jameson calls a few times while I wait, but I send the calls to voice mail. No doubt I'm whipping him into a frenzy by not answering, but will he care as much when he finds out I'm his sister?

If I'm his sister.

If.

I cling to the tiny word like it's my life raft in a stormy sea.

My phone vibrates with a notification and I can't help but check it. The Dealer has posted another photo. I half expect it to be a snap of me vomiting all over the West casino bathroom. But it's simply a photo of the Belle Mère Medical Clinic.

Whoever is behind this account knows exactly how to salt the wound. I look at the picture wondering if that place will be my deliverance or my damnation. I stare for so long that it blurs in and out of focus, and in the process, draws my attention to something I might not have noticed before.

The photo was taken from a car window. The Dealer must have been in a hurry to get this out, because a bit of the driver's side mirror is in the shot. I zoom in on the picture until the fragment comes into focus.

I nearly drop the phone, but somehow I keep it in my trembling hands long enough to send one text.

I know who you are.

A knock on the door startles me, and I stand, smoothing my shirt as if I'm going to impress May while smelling like vomit. When I open the door,

I'm met by familiar, if surprised eyes. The shock mirrored in them quickly shifts to anger.

Stepping to the side, I hold out my arm. I might not have expected May to be someone I know, but the pieces start to click together. "Won't you come in, Monroe?"

Read the final book in the Gilt Trilogy now!
ALL FALL DOWN

Everyone has a secret

But not for long…

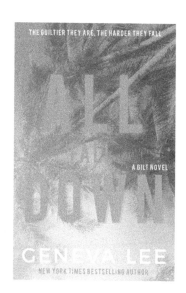

Acknowledgments

A special thanks to my team who keeps me going: Elise, Louise, Jessica, and Stephanie. Thank you isn't enough!

To my girls who always have my back, I love you.

To Kyla for claiming Jameson immediately.

To Mr. Lee for sharing me with other (fictional) men.

And to you for reading!

CPSIA information can be obtained
at www.ICGtesting.com
Printed in the USA
FSHW021731181118
53833FS